TOM CLANC

*Don't miss any o...
starring the te.... of Net Force ...*

VIRTUAL VANDALS

The Net Force Explorers go head-to-head with a group of teen-age pranksters on-line—and find out firsthand that virtual bullets can kill you!

THE DEADLIEST GAME

The virtual Dominion of Sarxos is the most popular war game on the Net. But someone is taking the game very seriously ...

ONE IS THE LONELIEST NUMBER

The Net Force Explorers have exiled Roddy—who sabotaged one program too many. But Roddy's created a new "play-room" to blow them away ...

THE ULTIMATE ESCAPE

Net Force Explorer pilot Julio Cortez and his family are being held hostage. And if the proper authorities refuse to help, it'll be the Net Force Explorers to the rescue!

THE GREAT RACE

A virtual space race against teams from other countries will be a blast for the Net Force Explorers. But someone will go to any extreme to sabotage the race—even murder ...

END GAME

An exclusive resort is suffering Net thefts, and Explorer Megan O'Malley is ready to take the thief down. But the criminal has a plan—to put her out of commission—*permanently* ...

TOM CLANCY'S
NET FORCE™

CYBERSPY

CREATED BY

Tom Clancy and **Steve Pieczenik**

BERKLEY JAM BOOKS, NEW YORK

TOM CLANCY'S NET FORCE: CYBERSPY

A Berkley Jam Book / published by arrangement with
Netco Partners

PRINTING HISTORY
Berkley Jam edition / November 1999

The Penguin Putnam Inc. World Wide Web site address is
http://www.penguinputnam.com

ISBN: 0-425-17191-4

BERKLEY JAM BOOKS®
Berkley Jam Books are published by The Berkley Publishing Group,
a division of Penguin Putnam Inc.,
375 Hudson Street, New York, New York 10014.
BERKLEY JAM and its logo
are trademarks belonging to Penguin Putnam Inc.

PRINTED IN THE UNITED STATES OF AMERICA

10 9 8 7 6 5 4 3 2 1

We'd like to thank the following people, without whom this book would have not been possible: Bill McCay, for help in rounding out the manuscript; Martin H. Greenberg, Larry Segriff, Denise Little, and John Helfers at Tekno Books; Mitchell Rubenstein and Laurie Silvers at BIG Entertainment; Tom Colgan of Penguin Putnam Inc.; Robert Youdelman, Esquire; and Tom Mallon, Esquire; and Robert Gottlieb of the William Morris Agency, agent and friend. We much appreciated the help.

TOM CLANCY'S NET FORCE™

CYBERSPY

I

Leif Anderson blinked, and the world reformed around him—literally. That blink had been his entry into the Net, the cyberrealm of the world's connected computers. Although he could see a room full of people all around him, that was a virtual construct. His physical body was still in New York City, reclining on his computer-link couch.

But he was attending a meeting of the Net Force Explorers, hosted by a computer somewhere in the Greater Washington metropolitan area.

This Tuesday he'd linked in a little early—maybe *too* early, Leif suddenly realized. The place was still filling up. This meeting was taking place in a typical government-issue virtual reality. Four blank walls, a floor, and a featureless expanse of ceiling—no frills, but it got the job done. Leif noticed one clever programming gimmick—the walls seemed to expand imperceptibly, so there was always the same amount of floor space around the ever-increasing crowd as more Explorers linked in.

Leif began paying attention to the growing mob. Judging by eyeball, they'd reached the usual number of kids for a meeting. But more kept coming. At this rate there would be a couple of thousand bodies on hand, logging in from all over the country.

Lots of kids he knew never missed a national meeting—you could always attend, if you had a Net-linked computer. All you needed was the time.

That wasn't something Leif could always afford. As the sixteen-year-old son of a mega-successful business tycoon, he had to face the demands of tough schooling as well as some business-related travel and meetings with his father, who felt that his son should know something about the family business. And then, of course, Leif had to maintain his reputation as a young playboy-in-training.

But when he found a message from Mark Gridley in his virtmail last night, suggesting that this meeting would be out of the ordinary, Leif had immediately cleared his schedule.

To judge by the still-growing crowd, a similar message must have gotten out to a lot of people.

Stretching up to his full height, Leif began scanning the crowd, looking for people he knew. Usually, he was the first to be spotted. That was the advantage—or drawback—of having a head of blazing red hair.

Even as he squinted, trying to catch a glimpse of someone, it occurred to him that he wasn't taking full advantage of the situation. This meeting was in virtual reality, after all. A lopsided grin crossed Leif's features as he pulled out his wallet. He flipped through credit cards and IDs until he came to the icons he'd stored in his virtual wallet. Each icon represented a potentially useful computer program that he'd created or purchased, all aimed at making his life a little easier as he surfed the Net. He selected a small lightning bolt, visualized the person he was looking for, then tossed the icon into the air. It grew in size and brilliance as it shot across the room, leaving a glowing trail behind it, and stopped over a small group of boys, pointing downward and emitting a greenish light.

In the middle of the group a tall black kid looked up, saw the lightning bolt above his head, and visually traced the trail it had left behind to its source.

The boy waved, and Leif could see a quick flash of teeth as the other boy grinned.

"Come on over!" David yelled. "I've been wandering around, trying to collect our crew."

Leif grabbed the beam of light his program had created, and gave it a tug. Next thing he knew, he was standing beside his friend. He left the glowing icon in place. This wasn't the first time he'd used this little program, so his friends knew what that bolt of lightning meant—"gather here, guys." Already, he could spot a couple of other familiar faces homing in on them, working their way through the crowd. Andy Moore's thatch of blond hair was almost as distinctive as Leif's—sometimes even more distinctive, since it always seemed to need a comb and a trim. It gleamed in the flashing light from the bolt as Andy headed their way. Matt Hunter had hitched up with P. J. Farris. They both waved. Megan O'Malley didn't bother with the niceties of virtual reality. She simply showed up by Leif's side and pointed at the bolt.

"I think your toy has served its purpose," she said. "Why not put it away before we all go blind?"

Leif shrugged and reached up for the icon. Its flashing light was distracting, he had to admit. At his touch the bolt shrank and dimmed, turning back into a wallet-sized icon. He tucked his program away, ready to be used again when he needed it.

"Hey, guys, wait for me," a familiar voice said.

Leif hadn't spotted Mark Gridley until he spoke up. He was a good three to four years younger than anyone else in the group was—and he was short for his age.

"Oh, hi, Squirt," Leif said.

"*So* glad you could make it," the boy said, with a touch of irony. Mark's face, tanned tawny by the Washington sun, was burnished just now by a dull red color. He hated to be called Squirt. Everyone knew that—but nearly everyone called him that anyway. The name just fit him perfectly.

The Squirt was a dangerous combination—a cocky little kid who happened to be a computer wizard. Give him a machine, and he could make it do just about anything.

Leif wasn't worried, though. Mark was good-natured enough about the nickname. He hadn't retaliated . . . so far.

•

"So what's so cool about this meeting?" Leif asked him. "I expected something more than a bit of cyber-showboating. The expanding room is nice, but it's not 'drop-everything' important."

"How about this?" Mark stepped into the middle of the friends' circle, sweeping around as if he were a fashion model.

Over his shorts and T-shirt he wore an adult-sized vest, which hung almost to the boy's knees. But even Leif's eyes were caught by the scintillating, swirling light show that glittered on the garment.

It wasn't light reflecting off beads, but rather a glow that came from within the material. Brilliant dots of gold, green, red, and blue moved in strange harmony, like traffic patterns seen from high above a city. The more Leif looked, the more colors he made out, racing around, shifting, creating kaleidoscopic patterns, then dissolving into seeming chaos.

"What do you think?" Mark asked, taking in their stunned faces with some satisfaction.

"Are you in a school play?" Matt asked. "That's a real coat of many colors."

"No, it's multipurpose camping gear," Andy teased. "You can wear it as a coat during deer season, use it as a tent, and play in traffic without your mom worrying about you."

Mark looked around the group, outrage warring with disbelief in his expression. "You guys are kidding me, right? You have to know what this is." He slapped the vest that hung on him. "This is the sharpest part of the cutting edge: Hardweare—the computer you wear!"

Of course they knew. They were having a little fun with the Squirt. Hardweare was all over the media this summer—the hottest new techno-toy for the trendy rich and corporate moguls. You couldn't see an executive on a holo-program— news, drama, or sitcom—without seeing one of the glittering vests. They were billed as the ultimate portable computer.

Leif finally took pity on the kid. "My dad priced one of those things and thought it was too much." Although, Leif had to admit, his father was thinking of buying into the company. "You must have really busted up the piggy bank—or was there a discount because they couldn't get you one that fit?''

Mark looked a little embarrassed. ''Actually, it's for my dad—he's evaluating it.'' Leif nodded. That made sense. Mark's father was the head of Net Force. Since his job was fighting crime on the Net, he would see any new technology as a matter of course. And, equally likely, the family's young genius would have a chance to play with it.

''How do you input?'' Megan wanted to know.

''Thought is the easiest,'' Mark replied. ''But you can talk to it, too. This sucker works with the natural electrical conductance of your skin. The vest will even access your computer surgical implants directly, no need to line up the laser. Everything just feeds in, like you're in a computer implant chair.''

The kids nodded. Having computer neural circuitry implanted behind their ears was one of the milestones of growing up—it meant you were ready for school. Most computers interacted with this circuitry by lining up the implant with a laser while the user sat in a specialized computer console chair or couch. But if the Hardweare computer was already in contact with your nervous system through your skin, that whole setup wouldn't be necessary.

''Right now I'm using a wireless interface to be here,'' Mark boasted. ''I'm standing in my living room, free as a bird, making the connection to the Net without an implant chair, or a vidphone, or anything, and the Hardweare computer is linking me to the Net through my implant and bouncing the signals to a satellite.''

''So you're standing—where did you say? In your living room?—while you link in with us?'' Megan asked.

Mark nodded proudly.

''So you're just standing out there, no computer-link couch, no closed door.'' Megan frowned. ''Don't you have a bunch of cats at your house? I'd expect them to love those dancing lights on your vest.''

Mark's eyes suddenly got a faraway look, as if he'd just caught a sound no one else could hear. ''Theo!'' he cried desperately, then vanished.

Leif began to laugh. He'd visited the Gridley house, and had met Theo—a large, yowly, blue-eyed Siamese cat . . . who'd never been declawed.

A very different Mark popped back into the room. His hair was tousled, his clothes rumpled, and he no longer wore the Hardweare vest. Mark's face was flushed, as if he'd been chasing something—or as if he'd been chased. And his right arm had four thin white scratches running down his forearm from his elbow.

"So what happened to your image here—is that another new fashion statement?" Leif asked. "A pin-striped tan?"

Mark looked embarrassed. "Theo was hanging on to my elbow when I got back. I guess that's how cats rappel for a quick getaway."

"Nice going, Squirt," Andy said. "That's a pretty neat trick. I take it this is your real-world appearance? How does your computer proxy reflect real-time changes in the way you look without you having to stop and program them in? I mean, I can't believe you'd want to advertise what happened to you—not on purpose. . . ."

Mark looked down at his disheveled state. "It didn't exactly work out the way I'd planned," he admitted. "A few months ago I programmed the house computer to continuously update my computer image based on my real appearance. We've got security system holo-monitors in nearly every room of the house, and they're always getting pictures of me. If I'm at home and within range of a camera, what I look like in real life is what I look like in virtual reality. If I'm not within range of a camera, the proxy defaults to my most recent available appearance."

"I'm not sure I'd like that," Megan said. "It's rough enough to have bad hair days in the real world without dragging them into veeyar with me."

"If you can share the coding, I'd definitely be interested in a copy," Leif said.

"I won't let you get your greedy mitts on my idea," Mark said, with a grin on his face. "You'd pass it on to your dad to make another couple of zillions."

"You certainly upstaged my news," David said. "It looks like I'm going to work for Hardweare."

"No way!" Matt exclaimed.

"The guy who founded the company only just turned nineteen," David replied. "He wants to give young programmers a chance."

"They're calling it the Young Genius Corps." Mark couldn't hide the jealousy in his voice. "But you've got to be at least fifteen to be considered."

David shrugged in embarrassment.

As if he weren't the young genius he actually was, Leif thought with a smile.

"They got on to me through the simulations of old space stuff I've programmed," David went on. "Those old-time mission programmers just about had to write code on the head of a pin. The computers in their probes were—well, *limited* is the nicest word I can come up with."

"I guess the system architecture for these Hardweare computers probably needs tight coding, too," Matt said.

"That's great!" Leif congratulated his friend. "Now that's a reason to attend this hoedown!"

"That wasn't why I messaged you, though," Mark piped up. "There's—"

Before he could explain, the meeting began. A moment ago all four walls of the room had been featureless. Now one wall grew back to accommodate a small stage—and the tall, spare man standing on it at parade rest. Even in civilian clothes, Captain James Winters looked every inch the Marine officer he'd once been.

"Welcome to the national meeting of the Net Force Explorers, August 12, 2025," the captain intoned. That was the official opening. Everything from here on would be recorded.

After the usual organizational stuff, the captain departed from the typical meeting agenda. "I have an announcement to make," he said. "Maybe some of you have heard that Net Force has been getting a lot of corporate complaints lately about hacking."

"So what else is new?" Andy muttered. "The bean counters won't shell out for security, so people get into their systems. Then the companies come crying to the government to protect them.''

Leif just shrugged. He agreed with Andy—corporate computers were safest when they were carefully protected. On the other hand, it was the job of Net Force to keep crime off the Net. If there was an upsurge in hacking, Net Force—and the Net Force Explorers—should take an interest.

''The reason I'm mentioning this in an open meeting is the *kind* of hacking we've been getting complaints about,'' Winters went on. ''The targets seem to be company secrets. Today we got a call from a soda company . . . which will remain nameless. They found the formula for their biggest-selling soft drink—a secret for more than 130 years—plastered around the Net. Not to mention the fast-food company who found the ingredients for their secret sauce posted worldwide.''

The Explorers laughed, but the captain didn't join in. ''More seriously, information leaked from an investment bank blew up a major takeover attempt, and several people in the insurance business may end up going to jail because certain supposedly secret files got out. These files show that some companies have been cheating the public.''

He looked across the room full of young people. ''Does anybody see a connection, other than the obvious one of secrets being revealed?''

There was a buzz of quiet discussion, but none of the Net Force Explorers offered a suggestion. Captain Winters nodded. ''To me, the very randomness of the revelations makes for a pattern. This isn't journalism, consumerism, or any kind of political-ism at work. It's not targeted at all. It's somebody digging up stuff that's hard to get, then flinging it around to show how smart he or she is. Maybe it comes from the kind of people I've been working with over the past few years''— Winters cast a stern eye over the kids in the room—''but I have come to identify behavior like that.''

He paused for a moment. ''It seems to me that we're not dealing with an adult here. I'm convinced this is a kid hacker—some kind of young genius who doesn't necessarily care what he turns up, as long as it shows off his or her cleverness.''

Leif couldn't help it. He glanced over at Mark Gridley. But the Squirt was standing on tiptoe, trying to get a look at Captain Winters, eagerly following every word.

"Because I suspect this hacker is a young person, I asked for permission to notify the Net Force Explorers and ask for your help in developing leads." Captain Winters's face grew grim. "Whoever is pulling this isn't just in trouble with the law. They could be in physical danger. Those insurance executives facing fraud charges would gladly have killed the person who gave them away. There are lots of other companies with equally dirty secrets—and they'd silence potential whistle-blowers the way you would squash a bug."

He looked around the suddenly silent group. "I don't need to remind you that the Explorers is an educational group—you have no police powers."

Leif grinned. In spite of the fact that they weren't actual agents, he and his friends had occasionally become involved—very involved, in fact—in active cases.

"What I'm asking for is information only—*no investigations, please!* What you don't know could kill you."

Was it Leif's imagination, or was the captain looking over at his little group? Something told him he wasn't just making up Winters's interest. The last time they'd gotten involved in an active case, it nearly *had* cost them their lives. . . .

2

"Young genius . . ."

The words seemed to echo in David Gray's memory as he stared out at the Maryland countryside flowing by the rear windows of the limo. The words might have been designed to describe Luddie MacPherson, the founder and president of Hardweare, Inc.

Inventing the computer-vests hadn't been enough. MacPherson had successfully patented his design, a far more difficult process. Getting a patent from the government meant submitting clear instructions and schematic drawings of any proposed invention. The papers had to be good enough to produce a working prototype utilizing new technology. The problem there, at least for the inventor, was that patented ideas could easily be stolen by nosy competitors if they could get their hands on the patent application, which, given the public nature of the documents, wasn't that hard to do. The real inventor could sue, of course, and usually did, but patent cases tended to drag on forever in the courts and were sometimes won by the person who could hire the toughest lawyers, rather than by the person who actually did the inventing. So there was a fine balance between giving away enough information to get a patent and giving away so much that anybody with a set of the schematics could make the finished product perfectly. These days a clever inventor always withheld a few things that contributed to the finished product when applying for a patent. Of course, any features that weren't covered in the patent application were also not covered by the resulting patent—but sometimes being effective at business was all about taking risks. Luddie MacPherson's patent applications gave him a square lock on his technology and, at least so far, had left any would-be copycats scratching their heads.

At the age of seventeen and a half MacPherson had shown himself to be an incredibly sharp businessman as well as a techno-wiz. And in less than two years he'd become a major player in the computer world.

That was about all that David had found on the Net about his prospective employer. He felt a little nervous entering this final interview with so little to go on.

But he had to hand it to Luddie MacPherson. How many companies sent chauffeured limousines out to pick up job seekers for their final interviews?

The initial weeding-out stages had been handled by Hardweare executives—guys in their twenties who'd impressed David with their technical know-how and their almost fanatical dedication to the company and their boss. As usual nowadays, those contacts had taken place over the Net. Apparently, however, Luddie MacPherson liked personal contact during the last stages.

From hints dropped by the executive assistant making his arrangements, David must have been an easy job. Most of the other aspirants were flying in for their interviews.

David leaned back against upholstery that felt too plush against his back. Maybe Leif Anderson could take this in stride. But for David, a cop's kid from downtown D.C., the level of luxury was a little too much. But it seemed that nothing was too good for Luddie MacPherson's Young Genius Corps.

Young genius . . . there was that phrase again.

David Gray didn't feel like a young genius. He would admit to having a good touch with computers, to being able to solve programming problems that baffled others—even professional programmers. But if this interview went right, he'd be working with some of the best minds—and sneakiest hackers—his age.

Just assembling this group showed Luddie MacPherson's unorthodox thinking. Some companies—especially those involved with computer security—used the more notorious hackers as consultants to probe for clients' security problems, and sometimes even to find weaknesses in their own security setups. But they didn't hire them to work within the company.

Hardweare did. Their recruiting program offered selected young programmers top-grade machinery and a chance to hone their skills on the sharpest part of technology's cutting edge. What the company got in return was excellent programming— and the chance to spot the next Luddie MacPherson.

Either the guy is incredibly *generous,* David thought, *or he wants a line on possible competition before it even starts to blossom.*

David himself didn't know exactly what he wanted to do with his talents. He'd thought of law school, but he'd also been fascinated by space. In veeyar simulations he'd shown the necessary abilities—physical and astrogational—to pilot spacecraft. And recent events had uncovered a certain flair for investigation. Maybe it was his cop heritage showing, but Net Force could always use sharp technologists.

But all those career decisions could wait. He was still a kid—he had years to go before he had to make up his mind. And in the meantime he would see how he measured up against the rest of the best and brightest. If he got a consulting job, Hardweare paid top dollar. Which was sure to help if he didn't get the scholarships he needed. Whatever he decided to do with his life, college was sure to cost a ton. And his dad's salary as a cop wasn't going to cover it.

He sighed, squirming back against that too-soft seat. Better not think that way. He didn't want to go into this meeting feeling half-defeated.

Just for a second in the rearview mirror David thought he caught a grin on the face of the driver. But he couldn't see the man's eyes under their dark sunglasses, and he could have been mistaken.

This guy must ferry a lot of hopefuls to the head office, David thought. *Who knows? Maybe this whole over-luxurious setup was some sort of test, to shake me up before seeing the big cheese.*

David turned from the driver to the view again. They seemed to be light-years instead of miles from downtown Washington. This was far from the beltway that girdled D.C. For David's taste, the buildings were too far apart—there was too much green, too many trees.

The limo slowed, leaving the main road. They seemed to slip back in time, rolling along a winding country lane. On one side David saw a white split-rail fence with a field beyond. There was no view on the other side—it was cut off by a high fieldstone wall.

Horses roamed in the green pastures. An eager colt began running beside the fence, racing the limo. David was so busy watching, he was caught by surprise when the big car slowed and began to turn away from the pasture and toward the stone wall. Where had those big iron gates come from?

The driver braked sharply in front of the massive gateway, beside one of the huge stone pillars flanking the entrance. A metal box was set in the stone with a large holo pickup sweeping back and forth over it. The pickup froze, studying the car. As David looked more closely, he could see multiple cameras inset in the fence as far as the eye could see, all of them carefully hidden, nearly invisible until he looked for them. He imagined that there was plenty of other security equipment scattered throughout the grounds—motion sensors, pressure plates, and other high-tech stuff he didn't even know about, much less know what to look for. This setup went way beyond a simple burglar alarm system.

Removing his sunglasses, the driver leaned out of the window to give the holo pickup a good view of his face. "If you wouldn't mind, Mr. Gray?"

David scooted across the seat to the left-hand window. By the time he got there, the window was down. He stuck his face out, watching as the driver placed his hand against a glass plate on the box.

Visual ID and palmprint.

Then it was David's turn. He presented his hand and face to the scanners, though he had no idea what his prospective employer planned to compare the scans to. Then the driver backed the car up to present himself to the holo pickup again. What did they want now?

The driver leaned forward, muttering something into a grille inset in the box. A password? A voiceprint? A DNA analysis of molecules in his expelled breath?

David found himself glancing nervously around. What did Luddie MacPherson have to back up such an elaborate system? Armed guards? Computer-controlled artillery?

In complete silence the big black bars swung open. The limo passed through, and David glanced at the gates. Something caught his eye—from any distance at all, they looked like fancy wrought iron. But up close, where the uncorroded glint of premium metal could be seen in a few small scratches and chips in the paint, it was clear that those suckers were made of solid stainless steel. It would take a reasonable amount of C-4 or a lot of time and a high-end blowtorch to get through them.

The gates closed as silently as they had opened, but David couldn't shake the image of prison bars swinging shut. Either Luddie MacPherson was very fond of his privacy, or he thought he had some serious enemies.

The limo moved along a crushed-shell driveway that cut through a manicured lawn toward a low fieldstone mansion. The vast field of green was obviously carefully tended, but the sort of landscaping David expected to see on grounds like this was noticeably absent. Nothing more than three inches high grew inside the walls. Looking at the flat expanse of greenery, David remembered Captain Winters talking about military tactics and zones of fire.

After bringing the car smoothly to a stop, the driver hopped out to get David's door. Looking at the man with new eyes, David detected a bulge in the driver's suit jacket—under the left armpit. The guy was carrying a gun!

David stepped out of the car. "Thanks for an . . . interesting ride," he said.

The driver responded with another lightning grin. Then he

glanced at the front door of the mansion, and David turned. Thick oak strapped with black iron, the door would have looked at home on a medieval castle. But it swung inward as silently as the gates, leaving a dark-haired, petite girl about David's age framed in the entranceway. She was pretty in a sort of exotic way, reminding David of HoloNet actresses portraying French girls, and she was wearing a Hardweare vest that fit her perfectly.

The girl beckoned. "I'm Sabotine MacPherson," she said. "Luddie will be with you in a minute."

David stepped inside, and the door swung shut without anyone touching it. Sabotine shrugged. "Luddie saw an old flatscreen TV show where the doors did that trick," she said. "When he found a company that could duplicate the arrangement . . ." She shook her head. "My brother buys into all sorts of strange technology."

Sabotine led the way from the stone entrance hall through an arched hallway painted to look like the sky, complete with clouds.

David saw paintings, sculptures on shelves, art objects in niches so they looked as if they were floating in air. He couldn't tell how they were lit—that was something beyond the cutting edge of high tech. But the artworks were all masterpieces . . . and all hand-worked.

They came to a living room or parlor—David didn't know what to call it. Sabotine sat down on a deceptively simple-looking wooden stool, gesturing to a leather couch nearby. As soon as the cushions detected David's weight, some sort of mechanisms deep within the piece of furniture were activated. It was as if the couch were a big animal snuggling him into the most comfortable position.

David squirmed, not comfortable at all, and caught Sabotine's apologetic smile. "Another technology your brother bought into?" he asked.

She nodded. "I try to keep him from taking our home completely into the twilight zone."

The room showed the same sort of strange conflict as the rest of the house David had seen—one-of-a-kind pieces of handmade furniture beside stuff that was almost bizarrely high-tech. Sabotine brushed a hand over the flashing Hard-weare vest she wore, and the lighting in the room changed, darkening except for a pair of spotlights circling where they sat.

David's attention, however, was caught by the rest of her outfit. It was some kind of natural fabric—maybe a sanded silk—and it was obvious that Sabotine hadn't picked it up in any mall. The garment's perfect fit spoke of hand tailoring.

"You try to balance the technology with all the handi-crafts?" David asked.

Sabotine nodded. "There's something . . . soulless about machine-made stuff. Once upon a time I made all my own clothes—before Luddie recruited me into his software division." She laughed at David's expression. "Yeah, I'd be your boss. You're doing fine—asking all the right questions."

David rolled his eyes. "Except the important one—why you were here to meet me."

"Sorry to be so late," another voice interrupted.

David turned to see Luddie MacPherson enter the room. Sabotine's older brother was a complete physical contrast to her—big, blond, and beefy. Judging by photographs from his rare public appearances, Luddie MacPherson often went with-out a tie. But as he stepped forward, wiping his face with a towel, the boy genius seemed to be taking the look a bit fur-ther.

Luddie MacPherson wasn't wearing a shirt. All he had on was a sweaty pair of exercise shorts . . . and the seemingly inevitable glittering Hardweare vest. The twinkling design of this one seemed to have a lot of red in it, David noticed.

"My workout ran a bit longer than I anticipated," Luddie said. "Hope you don't mind." He slapped his stomach. "Two years ago I was living on Ho-Hos and orange-cream soda. I've come a long way"—he grinned, plucking at the vest-computer, whose colors seemed to be calming down—"with this as my personal trainer. Sabotine programmed in every-thing I'd need to know about pumping myself up. I don't even have to think about it. While the computer was taking my body through all the reps, I was in virtual reality watching Shake-speare—right on the stage!"

Luddie struck a dramatic pose. " 'O, how bitter a thing it is to look into happiness through another man's eyes!' That's Orlando from *As You Like It*.'' He grinned, suddenly self-conscious. "I guess I pursued technology to the exclusion of almost everything else. Now I have the chance to catch up on all sorts of stuff while doing my exercises. Since the vest is already hooked into my nervous system, it monitors my pulse, blood pressure, respiration . . . it can even detect when I'm on the point of pushing too hard and giving myself a training-induced muscle sprain or strain, and stop me before I hurt myself. How many personal trainers can anticipate that—*and* also give you a classical education?''

"Yeah, yeah, it's wonderful." Sabotine waved him away. "Too bad it can't spot for you during weight training"—she wrinkled her nose, waving faster—"or tell you when you should've taken a shower.''

Luddie MacPherson swiped the towel along his arms. "Still a geek," he said, embarrassed. "It takes more than a computer and a couple of years to create a Renaissance man.''

David found himself grinning. "I've been in gyms before. I know what it smells like.''

"But it's not supposed to smell the same way in a gracious salon.'' Sabotine shook her head, smiling. "That's what happens when you try to run a personal life and a business in the same mansion.''

"Come on," Luddie said, leading the way out of the room. At the far end they had to detour around a life-sized sculpture. A female figure that looked remarkably like Sabotine seemed literally to be pulling herself out of a base of jagged rock. Luddie caught David looking. "She throws a lot of money at artists," he muttered as he brought them down a hallway. A pair of doors swung open as he approached, revealing an almost featureless space. It seemed to be carpeted, walled, and ceilinged in a strange silvery-gray fabric that gave pliantly under their feet.

"Welcome to the rubber room," Luddie announced cheerfully, heading straight for a small alcove David had initially missed. Hanging from a bar was a selection of Hardweare vests. "The effect is best if you get a good fit.'' He ran a practiced eye over David. "I'd figure you for a size forty long."

Wordlessly David nodded.

Luddie grinned. "If this computer thing craps out, I can always go into menswear."

David took off his jacket and shrugged into the vest, buttoning it up. A creepy tickling sensation, like his hair standing on end, swept along the back of his neck, where the vest touched his skin. "Just the computer making its connection," Luddie reassured him. "With a little more development, I hope to make implants a thing of the past. I'd rather have a little chill along my neck than that static-between-the-ears feeling."

Luddie had another vest in his hand. He tossed it to the floor. "Come on," he said. "I'll take you on the guided tour."

Suddenly the vest began to grow—no, David realized, they were *shrinking*! That little chill had not only established the connection with his implant—it had moved him into virtual reality!

3

Now David understood the significance of the padded room. His actual body was probably flaked out on the yielding surface, even as his virtual self scrambled after Luddie Mac-Pherson.

"Come on," the young inventor said. "I've got this thing set to turn this from a molehill to a mountain faster than you'd believe—and I don't want to go rappelling because you didn't keep up with me."

They'd continued to shrink while Luddie had been speaking, and David could see what he meant. From their new point of view, the crumpled garment on the floor looked more like a hill. David tried to think himself to the top, a common virtual-reality solution to covering long distances quickly. He didn't budge. He tried thinking about flying—another method of getting around fast in veeyar. Nothing. And the vest just kept getting bigger. Since this was Luddie's scenario, David had to follow Luddie's rules for getting around. Clearly Luddie hadn't programmed in any shortcuts. It was probably some kind of weird test for prospective employees. Well, David was going to pass the test. He decided he'd better move fast and keep up with the inventor, or he was in for a very long walk.

Luddie ran to the gigantic vest and began climbing, with David right on his heels. The boy inventor seemed to have a specific destination in mind. David was glad someone had an idea of what was going on. They continued to shrink even as they scaled Mt. Hardweare—which was now definitely looking like a mountain.

After a while, however, the climb became oddly easier, because David had shrunk to a size where he could actually grab on to the fiber-optic filaments that made up the body of the vest. String-size, cord-size, cable-size . . . then they became about the thickness of the pipes on monkey bars.

Luddie MacPherson continued to clamber up a steep slope— actually the side of a crease in the fabric—until he almost reached a large round building. Again, it took David a moment to readjust his frame of reference. The structure was actually a button on the front of the vest.

Apparently, it was also Luddie's destination. He stopped climbing and pulled David onto a specific filament—which had now grown large enough for the boys to swing astride like a horse. The young inventor grinned at David. "Pretty good," he complimented. "Some Net hotshots I've met are more like computer-link couch potatoes. When I take them on this tour, they're terrified of the heights, they can't move fast enough, and they're afraid to take risks moving through the environment—the trip puts them on the verge of blowing a gasket."

David shrugged. "I have two younger brothers. They put me through worse every Saturday morning."

Luddie looked like something out of a cheap horror show. Green light welled up from the optical filament beneath them—one of the million dots of color that flowed around the Hardweare vest. He laughed, an everyday sound very much at odds with his ghastly green skin. "Relax. From here on in, we ride."

They were still shrinking. The fiber beneath them had grown to the size of a giant pipe, about the size of a sidewalk. Then it seemed less rounded under their feet—and about the width of a city street. Now it seemed almost flat, and David couldn't even see where it ended.

We must be microscopic by now, he thought. *I hope Luddie didn't write any amoebas or germs into this sim.*

The boys grew so small they sank into the substance of the filament, just as a new blast of light—red, this time—came along.

"Here's our ride now," Luddie said.

David almost cried out in surprise as he and the inventor were engulfed in a cloud of gleaming scarlet points of energy and carried along on the wave.

It took a brief struggle, but he managed to regain his poise. "So now we're part of the vest's light-show."

"The beads of light aren't just there for show, although they do make the vest look pretty," Luddie lectured as they flashed along at tremendous speed. "They represent information packets, shunted among various processing sites."

"Decorative as well as useful," David said.

Luddie laughed. "Exactly."

"And tons of processing sites." David looked sharply at his prospective employer. "Just how big a computer network have you got in here disguised as a vest?"

"*Very* good," Luddie MacPherson said. "Of course I can't answer that—it's proprietary. But I can assure you that, pretty much regardless of the complexity of the problem or program a user presents, I've got enough processors that they can band together to handle it. The challenge was to make everything flexible—the physical components, you know—both so the system will fit comfortably around the end user's body, and so the hardware and software work flexibly and adaptively on any problem the user gives them. This network, despite its complexity, is tight enough and fast enough to give quick results."

They passed into a maze-like structure, and the ride immediately became bumpier. "A microchip?" David hazarded a guess.

"One of several main processors," Luddie admitted as they were shunted violently through the printed circuitry. Besides being shaken up, David noticed that the red glow around them had intensified until it was almost painful.

"I know we're putting you through a bit of sensory overload," MacPherson apologized, "but this really is proprietary technology—and I don't want people getting any ideas about the actual architecture.''

David thought this was taking security a bit too far. ''Can't any competitor buy a Hardweare vest and invest in the necessary technology to take it apart and steal the design?'' David asked.

''Not if they want a working system,'' Luddie grimly assured him. They went through another area, this one too blindingly bright to make out details. ''I call this our insurance circuit. If it detects anyone monkeying with the vest, it blows the whole system.''

''Makes the computers hard to repair.''

''If you have a problem, you get a replacement,'' Luddie said. ''We're selling a luxury machine here, not some sort of run-of-the mill computer you can get at Circuits Maximus. Call it the difference between caviar and scooter pies. The systems are built in automated factories, untouched by human hands—or eyes. Nobody knows exactly how these gizmos go together, except for me.''

The young man grinned and tapped the side of his head. ''And there are more than a couple of details that never made it onto paper or a datascrip.''

''I guess that explains the security all around you,'' David said.

''Most of it's because of this crap about leaks,'' Luddie said brusquely. ''I *know* they're not coming from our computers. I designed the safeguards between our systems and the Net myself. We've got a physical lock, software, and circuitry.''

''A lock? You mean one of those submicro padlocks they used to put on the old floppy disks?''

Luddie gave David a superior look. ''Better.''

David wasn't about to disagree. Whatever surrounded them—energy field, light packet, bead of light—suddenly accelerated to warp drive.

''What—?'' David began.

''This part of the tour is over,'' Luddie explained. ''We're heading to one of the interface circuits.''

''This is the part that will make computer-link couches a thing of the past?''

"It's bidirectional and biological. Input and output through the natural electrical conductivity of the skin as well as through user implants," Luddie said. "People have been trying to do it for twenty years. I made it work."

The micro-scenery around them was now a featureless blur as they rocketed along. Ahead was a huge square of whiteness. David abruptly recalled a line he'd read in every cheesy description of an out-of-body experience: *"Head for the light."*

He didn't mention it, not sure how the joke would be taken—and, frankly, his mouth was a little too dry for talking. They swooped toward the square opening—some sort of receptor, David figured—and the glow enveloped them, a featureless pearly illumination.

David was reminded of a plane flight he'd taken, where the transcontinental jet had passed through a huge cloud bank. Beyond the porthole the world had been featureless, glowing whiteness, the sunlight filtered through millions of tiny ice crystals.

Then the haze thinned, and David wondered if the sim had somehow read his mind. They *were* in a cloud, or rather they'd been in a cloud. Now they had come out of it and were heading toward the ground—without an airplane, without even a parachute.

Free-falling from a couple of thousand feet would be enough to get anybody's adrenaline going. But David found himself nearly overwhelmed with terror as he dropped. His heart was thumping wildly, as if it were going to burst out of his chest . . . or just plain burst.

It's just a sim, he kept telling himself. *This is veeyar!* But as the ground came ever closer, the irrational panic gnawed away at him.

Every commercial virtual simulation had built-in safeguards to keep people from getting hurt. You could go skiing nude in a virtual blizzard without worrying about frostbite or broken legs—thanks to automatic pain blocks. Oh, some veeyar operators believed in punishing people for their simulated screwups. You might get a twinge of pain, even a zap. David did it himself. That's why some people were a little nervous about his space sims. Still, any serious pain was filtered out by the safeguards on the Net and by the users' own default settings for pain in their individual systems.

But Luddie MacPherson was a computer genius. And they *weren't* accessing the Net from David's own system. All this was almost certainly private, proprietary software operating in a closed system. Who knew what Luddy might have worked into this sim for their impact at ground level?

David wanted to ask, to make some sort of a comment. His friends always kidded him about being a bit *too* much on the cool side. But right now he could barely think, much less speak.

Wait—something's happening! David felt his body somehow stretching, expanding. His head remained about a hundred feet above the ground. But his feet grew down to make a gentle impact, actually sinking a little bit into the soft earth.

David blinked, trying to assimilate the lightning change of perspective. He'd just gone from a microbe's-eye view of the world to becoming a giant. Luddie MacPherson gestured expansively to the rolling farmland around them. "Some view, huh?"

"It was a little more . . . *intense* a couple of seconds ago," David replied.

"Sorry about that." The boyish inventor looked apologetic. "It was in the nature of psychological testing—to see how you handled stress."

David looked down at his pants. "Well, they don't *look* wet."

MacPherson laughed. "Very good." He pointed toward their feet. "This is one of my factories."

David squinted downward. "No windows?" The Hardweare manufacturing complex looked like a set of concrete blocks dropped in the middle of the green fields.

"None needed," he was assured. "The whole setup is automated." Luddie peeled back the roof on one of the featureless blocks. Antlike machines were busily at work churning out lines of vests which looked like periods from where David was standing. As for any secrets of the manufacturing process, they were too tiny for David to make out.

You've got to hand it to this guy, David thought. *He shrinks*

*me down too small to understand how the vest works. Then
he blows me up to keep me away from the way they're con-
structed.*

He noticed something else that didn't show at first in this
scale. "How thick are those walls?" he asked. "If Hitler had
fortifications like that in Normandy, we'd still be trying to get
a foothold in France."

Smaller boxes surrounded the factory buildings. These ones
did have windows—that looked more like loopholes. "Security?" David asked.

"I've got competitors who would love to see Hardweare
factories suffer . . . accidents," Luddie said flatly. "It's not so
different from what surrounds this house—although we're better landscaped."

He snapped a finger, and the rolling landscape turned into
the silver-gray carpeted splendor of Luddie MacPherson's
rubber room. David felt a tingling at the back of his neck.

The door swung open, and David swung warily to face it.
The surroundings matched the real-world room where they'd
started this little veeyar trip exactly. Were they back in the
real world? Was the sim actually over? Or were they still in
veeyar and was MacPherson about to throw a new curve at
him?

A deeply tanned guy about David's age breezed into the
room, a questioning look on his handsome face. "How'd it
go?"

"Here's the guy you can thank for the wild ride," Luddie
said. "David Gray, meet Nick D'Aliso."

David glanced in surprise at Nick's regular features.

"From that once-over, I take it you know my nickname—
no, it ain't based on my looks," Nick told him.

No one who was into computers could fail to hear stories
about Nick D'Aliso, alias "Nicky da Weasel." Although the
nickname sounded like something out of a bad Mafia movie,
it came from D'Aliso's hacking ability. He was able to weasel
his way into supposedly impregnable systems. Then, when he
finally got caught, he had weaseled his way out of trouble by
hiring out as a computer security expert.

If MacPherson hired this guy, he really is serious about

keeping his secrets under wraps, David thought. Considering the hacker's slippery business ethics, though, who would protect the secrets from Nicky da Weasel?

"Nick programmed everything you just went through in that sim," Luddie MacPherson explained. "It all came from the vest you were wearing—we never connected with the Net."

"Stand-alone computing—what a concept," David said.

"Our customers are willing to pay for privacy—even if all they're doing is running a sim."

Another way for rich, bored executives to waste their time, David thought. He thought back over his orientation tour and turned to Nick D'Aliso. "You must have had an interesting time of it coming up with some of that stuff. It really caught my . . . attention a couple of times." David couldn't forget the moments his heart had pounded with fear during the sim—fear all out of proportion to the situation.

"I hear you're pretty handy at getting attention yourself," Nick replied. "Is it true you won that space race competition out in Hollywood by running your end of the sim through a laptop computer?"

Before David could answer, Luddie turned the conversation back to business. "We need creative programmers. Our clients pay for and expect the best from us. No computer has the processing capacity to create infinite real worlds in a sim. That means we have to fool people's eyes—and minds. Have you ever heard the word *gestalt* before?"

"It's German, isn't it?" David said. "I've seen it in relation to psychology. Something about perceiving things or symbols as something more than the sum of their parts."

Luddie nodded. "Close enough. We have to make our sims more than the sum of their parts. For instance, in that tour, the landscape wasn't that remarkable. Neither was the system architecture."

"But you dropped me over one landscape and blew me through the other." David thought about his sudden panic attack. "You did something else as well, didn't you?"

"That's where I really got involved," Nick said. "I've been working on manipulating moods in veeyar through subliminal cues."

"Triggering emotions, you mean," David interjected, re-membering how he'd felt. "That was more than a mood I went through."

"It's not that much different from when the screechy violins start playing during a horror flick." Nick shrugged. "It's just a warning that scary stuff is coming. In this case, the warnings can't be sensed by your conscious mind, but we can get your heart thumping and your palms sweating. Every veeyar sim does it to some extent—it's what makes them fun. I'm just better at manipulating emotions through subliminal input than most programmers. Much better, in fact."

"We need something to give us an edge," Luddie said.

David thought it came uncomfortably close to brainwashing, but he didn't say anything.

"Nice to meet you," Nick said. He stepped toward the door, then swung back. "Oh, yeah, Luddie. Sabotine didn't want to disturb you during the sim. She asked me to ask if a rerun of the dinner we had last night was okay. I guess we've got lots of leftovers."

Nick D'Aliso was living with the MacPhersons?

A little of the surprise David felt must have shown on his face.

"Most of the work here is handled freelance, or by tele-commuting," Luddie said. "But if there's a hot project on, it's just as easy to move someone in. We've got lots of room, especially since there are no servants around."

Or maybe he just wants to keep an eye on the slippery Mr. D'Aliso, David added silently. *I certainly would.*

"It's a pretty big house, just for your family," David said.

"Just my sister," Luddie said abruptly. He looked at his watch. "Damn, got to run. Nick, you'll take care of David?"

Before David quite realized it, Luddie MacPherson was gone. Not even a handshake.

Nick D'Aliso gave him a sardonic smile. "You were doing pretty well until you mentioned family." He shook his head. "Luddie's family is a real sore point. Of course, it's not com-mon knowledge. The records are all in juvie court, and they're sealed. I take it you don't do much hacking? Because I'm sure you checked up on the MacPhersons before you came here."

"No," David said. "I try to not to commit any felonies when I'm interviewing for a job. But I'm aware that's not everybody's approach." Certainly not Nicky da Weasel's, if the rumors David had heard were true.

"It would have saved you real trouble here. Luddie had himself declared an emancipated minor. He divorced his family—had to, if he wanted to go full-speed ahead into computers. His father wouldn't let him."

"Wouldn't let him?" David echoed.

"His dad heads up the Manual Minority. You must have heard of them."

"The antitechnology movement."

"The lunatics who want to drag us back to the Stone Age," Nick contradicted. "Some of them would actually be happy if we were all living in caves—they seem to think they'd be among the ten percent of the human population that a natural ecology would support."

"Computers have remade our world—and in just one lifetime," David pointed out. "Working, communications, even entertainment . . . there've been a lot of changes to accommodate."

"Calling computers the devil doesn't sound much like accommodation to me," Nick replied. "That's what Battlin' Bob MacPherson told his troops at their last big meeting." As he led the way back to the mansion's front door, his expression suggested that David didn't need to worry about MacPherson family difficulties.

He'd never be working for Hardweare, anyway.

4

Leif Anderson looked sympathetically at David Gray—or rather, at the holographic image of David floating over his computer system. "So you don't think the interview went well?"

"Oh, it went fine—until the end." David told Leif about Luddie MacPherson's strange behavior—and Nick D'Aliso's explanation.

"Nicky da Weasel?" Leif interrupted. "This MacPherson guy goes top-drawer . . . or is this part of a plea bargain for D'Aliso?"

David shrugged. "From what I understand, he's in there to help with computer security—and doing some programming, as well."

"The guy has a rep for coming out on top of whatever situation he falls into," Leif said. "Could he possibly have been scamming you with that story?"

The expression on David's face was almost funny. "That's what I've been trying to find out. Nick implied there wasn't any information to be found using legal searches. Which, given that Luddie and his father—if Nicky is telling the truth and Battlin' Bob *is* Luddie's father—are both public figures, is pretty strange. But Nick's been right so far. I've been getting nowhere!''

"Come on," Leif said a little sharply. "Luddie MacPherson is a full-fledged celebrity. The simplest Net search—"

"Hasn't turned up squat about his personal life," David finished in a frustrated tone of voice.

"That's—" Leif bit back on the word *ridiculous*. David Gray took his computers very seriously and wasn't about to make a ridiculous announcement. "Tell me about it," Leif finally said.

David described how a general data request had grown considerably more specific, backed by some heavy-duty search engines. "I got lots of stuff about his business, press releases, statements about company moves and the future of technology—but nothing personal about him, nothing about his sister, and nothing about any relationship with Battlin' Bob MacPherson."

"But any decent newspaper archive should have that sort of background," Leif objected.

David gave him an exasperated look. "*The New York Times, The Washington Post*, and *The Wall Street Journal* all have the same response—'Information not available.' That's when I figured I'd better talk to you."

"Oho." Leif grinned at his friend's image. "Now the picture becomes clear. You aren't looking for sympathy. You want someone to finagle the information. Now, I'm no Nick D'Aliso."

"But you know people," David finished for him. "Besides, I thought this was the kind of mystery that would interest you."

"Curiosity killed that cat." Leif brushed a hand through his bright red hair, a broader grin lighting his sharp features. "But people tell me I look more like a fox. I'll give it a try. If anything interesting turns up, I'll buzz you back."

David disconnected, and Leif sat in silence for a long moment, contemplating his Net setup. He didn't have Nick D'Aliso's programming brilliance—or even David Gray's. What he did have was money, lots of it, thanks to his father. Between his dad's international business and a few of his own ventures, Leif had encountered some of the best hired guns in the programming trade. He'd also come across some oddball bits of information, which he'd squirreled away. Given his much-deserved reputation for loving a good, well-crafted scheme, Leif always tried to keep a surprise or two up his sleeve.

He sank back against a computer-link couch, wincing as he interfaced with his computer. A bunch of cyber-badboys—and girls—had once attacked Leif in veeyar. The result was a sensitivity around his implant circuits. Where others got the equivalent of mental static, he got what felt like a sharp pain in the brain.

When it passed, he was at his virtual desktop, a cluttered collection of three-dimensional icons which drove various programs. Leif picked up three glowing geometric shapes, pressing them in a certain order to open one of the desk drawers. They stuck in place, he murmured a password, and the drawer opened. Otherwise, it wouldn't.

Inside was a smaller collection of icons which he privately called his Cool Stuff—access codes most people couldn't get; beta-test programs which hadn't been released yet; unofficial software; quasi-legal bits of hacker work he'd come across or commissioned. Examining the cache, he selected several neat little bits of software . . . and then put most of them back. A single item remained in his hand. The key chain was a set of access codes he'd acquired from one of his more disreputable acquaintances. *"Information not available,"* huh?

"We'll see about that," he muttered. He closed the drawer and locked it again.

From the desktop he took a couple of search utility programs, then an icon shaped like a lightning bolt, and launched himself into the Net. Leif took a roundabout route to *The Washington Post*'s site. It stood like a skyscraper office building built of neon light, emblazoned with the paper's logo. This was a popular Net site, and tiny mayfly figures whizzed around it: fact-checkers, kids doing school assignments, historical researchers . . . Leif had heard there was even a group of fans who dropped in to read ancient comic strips from eighty and ninety years ago.

He entered the virtual construct, passing through crowded hallways—access areas for popular data dumps. As he got closer to his destination, however, the crowds thinned, until finally he had a hall of neon light all to himself. Unlike the public data areas, this corridor had no doorways—or rather, none would appear unless the researcher had the proper access codes.

Leif retrieved his key-chain icon and pressed it against the wall. He sighed in relief when an entrance appeared. The codes hadn't been changed. He stepped into a space that looked like a stylized picture of a file room—glowing file cabinets on all four walls. He'd penetrated the newspaper's restricted access files—although well toward the bottom of the *Post*'s security priorities. Leif was unlikely to stumble over the true name of Deep Throat, the guy who'd helped blow the whistle on the Watergate scandal, or any juicy information on assassinations or congressional wrongdoing.

But he could reasonably assume this was the place to verify not-so-hot gossip—like who Luddie MacPherson's parents might be. Leif activated one of his search utilities, instructing it to search for information on Luddie MacPherson.

But the instant he slapped the program against one of the file drawers, a nerve-shattering alarm erupted from all around him. The power of the neon lights grew excruciatingly intense, and the file cabinets disappeared. The file room walls were bare. From Leif's point of view, the biggest concern was that the door had disappeared. He could log off, of course, but he'd undoubtedly be traced. He hadn't taken precautions against it—he'd thought it wasn't necessary for something so simple. *Wrong, Leif.* And he hadn't even found a single useful piece of information.

Busted, he thought. *And I don't even know what I did.*

It took some fast talking—and some expensive talking from a lawyer Dad sent over—but the paper wasn't going to do anything to Leif for trying to access their restricted files. He did find himself on the receiving end of a few well-chosen words from his parents.

At last he sat alone in his room, facing his computer console. Of course, according to his parents, after this he wasn't supposed to use it for anything but homework until further notice. He leaned back in his computer-link couch, entered veeyar . . . and went straight for his drawer full of Cool Stuff.

One program took him on a course through the Net like a hyperactive pinball, making sure he couldn't be followed. It left him at what looked like a small generic office building— home to any of a million Net sites offering anything from salvation to sexy underwear. Leif entered, heading upstairs. Most of the enterprises were open to the public, but Leif's destination was a bit more selective.

He arrived at the end of the hallway and produced another program icon. It opened the door. Leif headed into a small office filled nearly to the bursting point with a cutting-edge computer console. Of course, it was a virtual device. But it was almost an exact duplicate of the computer Leif had used to enter cyberspace.

"Déjà vu all over again," Leif murmured, turning the virtual machine on.

The hologram projector on the computer came to life, displaying a face that looked as though it had been drawn by a three-year-old.

"Heard you got nailed at the *Post*." The voice had obviously been mechanically altered.

"I told them I got the access codes from a public bulletin board that doesn't seem to be there anymore," Leif said.

"Well, at least they didn't follow you here," the unnerving sketch-face told him.

"Do you always communicate through cutouts?" Leif asked.

"Safer," the crude drawing told him. "Especially when you're selling things that might annoy other people."

Like proxies that could ruin someone's virtual party, Leif thought. *Or access codes to supposedly secure newspaper archives.*

"I don't think you have anything to complain about," the hacker told him. "Your little stunt cost *me* money. They've changed all the codes at the *Post* site. I've lost a product. Why did you go after the MacPherson material? The papers are super-paranoid about hacking on those files, ever since the killbot thing.''

"Killbot?" Leif knew what they were—programs released on the Net to track down data on certain subjects—or people—and erase it. "Luddie MacPherson sent out killbots to wipe his personal life off the Net?"

The sketchy face nodded. "They've erased a lot of files— even in HoloNews. The papers and news services haven't got a word on him that isn't related to his business. I hear some places they're keeping the MacPherson file in hard copy only, and data's still gotten lost. The data fields that told people where the printed files could be found were erased."

"Is that legal?" Leif asked.

"It is, most places, if you're willing to pay enough for the privilege, or, failing that, willing to sue to keep the information out of the papers. Luddie was. You won't find an unofficial word about him in any searchable file on the planet."

"All that for a little privacy," Leif said.

"It was a sore spot for Luddie, suing to get out of his family. I knew the guy when he was working like a dog to raise money to get his sister loose. The father was a real piece of work—he wouldn't let the kids have neural implants put in when they went to school."

Leif remembered the form his parents had to sign—he'd always thought it was a formality. "So Luddie's father really *is* Battlin' Bob MacPherson?"

The sketch-face nodded. "Head of the Manual Minority. Look at what he named his kids! Luddie is named for the Luddites, an antitechnology movement from the 1810s—hand-weavers who destroyed weaving machinery. Sabotine gets her name from the saboteurs." The hidden hacker paused. "She was born to Battlin' Bob's second wife, a French woman. He married her because he thought Europeans were less obsessed with technology. But she left him, too."

Leif, however, skipped back to the phrase that interested him. "You actually know Luddie MacPherson?"

"*Knew* him," the hacker replied. "There was this group of hackers who used to hang around in this chat room. We all thought we were budding geniuses. But MacPherson was the real thing. You ever see this trick?''

A grid of twelve dots appeared in the holographic display:

"Now you've got to link the dots with only unbroken lines, one leading into the next."

"Okay." Leif stared for a moment, then extended a finger, leaving a line of fire as he went from dot to dot.

"That's one way," the hidden hacker approved. Then the connections Leif had drawn disappeared, leaving only the dots. "Now, using the same rules, can you do the same using only five lines?"

Leif frowned, staring harder at the pattern, tracing imaginary lines back and forth. "Can't be done," he said.

"But it can." A line of fire suddenly appeared, slashing through the bottom row of dots, running off the grid, then angling back to catch a few more dots, extending past the gridwork again, and veering back. When the hacker was done, there were indeed only five lines, but they made a weird pattern:

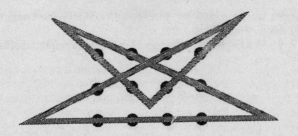

"I should have caught on when you said this was a trick," Leif said in disgust.

"It just illustrates a way of thinking," the hacker replied. "I can do some pretty cool things with a computer. So could the other guys in that chat room. We could connect the dots. But Luddie—he thought *beyond* the dots. And that led to some pretty amazing things."

The hacker sighed. "Even back then the ideas that came out of his head . . . We would hang around, talking, just blowing off electrons. Luddie would play with an idea, thinking out loud. Some other guys picked up on a couple of those—let's call them original suggestions—and made a heap of cash. I think that's when Luddie suddenly turned into Mr. Cutthroat. Or maybe it was the fight for his sister. He got seriously into making money, and the more he made, the more secretive he became."

All of Leif's previous dealings with this sketch-faced guy had been strictly business—and he'd been tough as nails. So it surprised Leif to hear a wistful note in the hacker's voice.

"I miss those times—getting together with an honest-to-God genius. When you think of what Luddie had to overcome . . . what could he have been if he'd had a normal upbringing. . . ."

Leif smiled. "He might have ended up in the Manual Minority. You said it yourself—kids turn out to be the opposite of their parents."

Kind of like a self-made billionaire fathering an aimless playboy of a son.

But Leif kept that thought strictly to himself.

The hacker got a bit more businesslike before they ended their meeting. Leif agreed to compensate him for his lost product, but the figure they agreed upon wasn't an outrageous amount. They both wanted to be able to deal together again in the future.

Leif cut out of veeyar and found himself back in his room.

Well, he thought, *thanks to those killbots I'm obviously not going to discover much about Luddie's family life on the Net, unless I'm willing to break the law instead of merely bending it. And I'm not. But maybe I can pick up a little on his old man. . . .*

He went to work.

Leif's Net search found plenty of information on the elder MacPherson. Battlin' Bob had started out as a professional wrestler, but left entertainment sports for an initially successful career in politics. He'd become an advocate on issues of privacy, which led in turn to the media, computers, and, finally, technology in general. MacPherson brought all his celebrity into the fight against machines, as well as a colorful personality and an unruly spirit which never gave up.

He needed all those assets to survive the jokes aimed at him. He was killed politically by cracks like "Jump on the MacPherson bandwagon—it's the one with stone wheels."

Battlin' Bob never got a lot of voters to back him, but he was embraced by the Manual Minority. Over the years he'd raised a lot of valid issues, led a lot of demonstrations, broken a few laws—and a few heads.

Leif was surprised to discover that the national headquarters for the group was in New York City. He'd have figured they'd go for some rural paradise. Then again, New York was still media central. Leif noted the address. It couldn't hurt to take a short walk in that general direction.

• • •

The next afternoon after school Leif strolled down Sixth Avenue. The Manual Minority's offices were located in a high-rise that had been the top of the line twenty years ago. Now it was going to seed, like so many office buildings in a world where most people telecommuted to work on their computers.

As he rose in the elevator, Leif wondered how many of the building's floors were empty, or simply given over to computer equipment-Net servers. From the way the car jerked and chugged up to the twenty-third floor, it might have been a better idea to check out the group from cyberspace.

But then, Leif didn't expect a big Net presence from a group that advocated getting rid of computers.

The elevator doors opened onto a reception area whose wooden paneling had seen better days. The wall behind the receptionist had a collection of drill holes and glue stains, left-overs from a succession of different company names and logos. It was currently empty of logos. Apparently, the Manual Minority felt no need to advertise.

As for the receptionist, well, she was pretty in a fierce sort of way, her burning brown eyes framed in a tangle of light-brown curls.

"How can I help you?" she asked.

"Is this the Manual Minority?" Leif made his voice sound especially timid and hesitant. "I've heard a little bit about this group and would like to learn more, if someone could answer questions."

"I think Mr. MacPherson is free," the girl said. "He always likes to talk to young people. Hold on a minute." She actually got up and went to check. Her desk didn't even have an old-style phone or intercom on it.

Leif couldn't believe his luck when the young woman returned in a moment and led him down a corridor. "He'll be right with you," she said, opening a door.

The office was empty, the carpet worn and faded except for rectangular sections where desks or computer consoles had once stood. There were holes in the walls, revealing wiring or plumbing or something.

Leif turned from his inspection as the door opened. A big, burly man entered, his blond hair going thin on top.

"What can I do for you, Mr. Anderson?" the man said.

Leif stared at MacPherson's craggy features. He hadn't given his name!

Leif took a step forward—then dropped to his knees, his hands gripping his temples.

5

Through a haze of pain Leif was barely aware of the man turning back to the door. "Kathy! Kill the induction circuits!"

The paralyzing agony ebbed away, and Battlin' Bob MacPherson helped Leif to his feet. "Are you all right?"

"Fine—except for that lingering feeling that someone tried to take off the top of my head with a butter knife," Leif replied. "What *was* that, anyway?"

"I suppose you could call it cyber-feedback," MacPherson said. "This office has been wired up to interact with implant circuitry. When the power's engaged, it gives a good jolt of static to any metalheads in the room."

Leif grimaced. "Metalhead? How nice to find that you folks have a contemptuous nickname for the computerized majority. And whatever database you assembled on me could have been more complete. I once suffered serious implant trauma after being attacked in veeyar."

"I apologize for causing you pain." Battlin' Bob raised a heavy eyebrow. "But doesn't your experience suggest certain drawbacks about your technology of choice?"

"What my current experience suggests is that the Manual

Minority uses a lot of the technologies it's supposedly against,'' Leif said grimly.

"How dreadful.'' MacPherson's voice took on a mocking tone. "We monitor who logs on to Manual Minority Net sites—or runs data searches on Manual Minority people. We always check such curious people out, especially when they're rich or famous.'' He paused. "And when we find somebody playing junior investigator for Net Force, we give them a warm welcome.''

"And you use computers to do it, machines which you claim to think are instruments of the devil.'' Leif looked the big man in the eyes. "And you use them to intrude on people's privacy—that's also something you personally find . . . nasty.''

MacPherson shrugged heavy shoulders. "Unfortunately, I find this the sort of fight where I have to use the enemy's weapons against him. You complain about what I did? My actions were possible because of the society which you and the rest of your so-called majority have created.''

"I think it's a little late for everyone to scrap all machinery and take up hunting and gathering,'' Leif said sarcastically.

"Some of the more radical members of the Manual Minority feel that way,'' MacPherson admitted. "Call them a minority within the minority. Most of us simply feel that we aren't merely being bombarded by technology anymore— we're being stampeded. You're technically up to date. Between your father's company and the Net Force Explorers, you probably see more up-and-coming technology than most. Don't you feel it's a little much sometimes?''

Sometimes Leif did feel that way, when some sort of advance suddenly made class material from a year ago totally obsolete. He didn't say anything out loud, but the big man must have read the answer in his eyes.

"You know, only a century ago, most technology could still be repaired at home by a reasonably handy amateur—the Model T Ford, the crystal radio, the electric lamp. Then machines were taken out of the hands of the average guy—the next generation of machines could only be repaired by trained service personnel. And in the nineteen eighties technology got so complicated people could hardly use the working machines in their homes anymore. You ever hear about the old VCRs?''

"The magnetic recorders for flatscreen TV," Leif said.

"Users had to set a clock inside each box if they wanted to record programs automatically. In many houses those clocks blinked endlessly at twelve midnight, because the owners couldn't figure out how to set them.''

"The beginning of the Manual Minority," Leif said.

"More like a majority. Then came computers, and a tremendous publishing boom in guidebooks with words like *idiot* or *dummy* in their titles. The same thing goes on now, except it's software.''

Leif nodded. Some of his father's fortune came from marketing so-called "dummyware" instruction programs. "Technology causes a problem, so technology solves the problem.''

"Or, to put it another way, we're being pulled along in a flash flood of technology without ever getting a chance to stand still and evaluate how this is shaping our future. Would people have rushed to embrace the automobile if they'd known in advance what suburbs would do to cities and small towns, or how extended families effectively vanished because people scattered all over the country? Television created the couch potato, and it's only getting worse with computers and veeyar—and I haven't even begun to talk about what's happened to people's privacy.''

"Would we be better off using horses and books?" Leif shot back. "The automobile was originally hailed as a solution to urban pollution. Think of what enough horses to handle current transportation needs would do to the streets and air of most cities. . . . And do you know how many forests were chopped down to print books, newspapers, and catalogs over the last two centuries before virtual reality made print on paper mostly obsolete? Technology isn't all bad. And we're not the only country in the world using it, you know.''

"Oh, yeah. When you're faced with a tough decision, blame the global economy.''

Leif began to see how Battlin' Bob got his name. But the big man went on.

"That argument has put big business more and more in

charge, not just of our economy, but of our lives. Especially now that we've turned information into a business product. People worried about credit and government borrowing— thought it was mortgaging our future. But we're *giving* that future away to large corporations who determine what we hear, what we know, and who tinker with the very food our farmers grow just so they can slap a patent and a logo on it.''

''Your son is creating a whole new take on computer technology—and he certainly doesn't have a *large* corporation,'' Leif argued.

Bob MacPherson's face went stony. ''Luddie MacPherson's creation is more subversive than most technology—I think it's more powerful than even he understands. And all I can do is hope he's not crushed as the big boys fight to take it over.''

There was nothing Leif could say to that. It had the ring of sterling truth to it.

Maybe David's lucky that he messed up the end of his interview, he thought. *From what I've seen of the family, they seem to be living examples of what a thin line separates genius and insanity.*

David Gray stared in astonishment at Luddie MacPherson's hologram image.

''It's your turn to say something,'' Luddie prompted. ''I just offered you a job.''

''I—I didn't expect that,'' David admitted.

''Let's just say you're a little easier to research than I am,'' MacPherson said. ''I like the fact that you're with the Net Force Explorers, even if Nick D'Aliso doesn't.''

''Why?'' David asked bluntly.

''There's a whole lot of screaming going on about secrets being leaked onto the Net,'' the young inventor said. ''I've got people on my neck, trying to blame the leaks on Hardweare. Either they're trying to bad-mouth a product that's kicking their butts, to try and force more information out of us so they can copy the vests . . . or to set us up for a takeover.'' MacPherson scowled. ''I *know* we're not responsible for this cyber-leak.''

''You told me that before,'' David said.

"I designed those suckers. I got them up and running. I know them like nobody else. As for what those people are claiming, there is no way it can happen."

Trust me, I'm the inventor, David thought, unconvinced.

"You might have an easier time getting people to believe you if you let them see how the vests work," David said. "Maybe Net Force—"

"No way," Luddie interrupted. "This isn't academic science, where you give out everything you did to see if others get reproducible results. If I do that, I'll be up to my ass in imitations."

The young genius shook his head. "I'm not going to give away our technological edge to prove we're innocent. But if I let in a connection with Net Force, no matter how tenuous, that should help our credibility with the agency. I mean, people will have to give us a chance to prove we're on the up-and-up." Luddie suddenly grinned. "Even if it does mean taking on somebody a little too goody-goody for Nick's taste."

David laughed. "Well, anything that annoys Nicky da Weasel can't be all bad."

"So you're taking the job?"

David thought the situation over—was he willing to go along with a public-relations gesture to work on the hottest computer technology to come along in years? This one seemed like a no-brainer. "Okay, you've hired yourself a goody-goody," David said, "on the understanding that if I do find any problems, Net Force will hear about them."

"You're not going to find anything," Luddie said confidently. "But I'll be happy to put that in writing. You'll have to sign some confidentiality stuff before coming on board—and I'll make sure that the language allows you to report to Net Force if you feel the need. I'll tell Sabotine you're joining the team. She'll get in touch with you."

That's right, David thought, *Sabotine is in charge of programming.*

Luddie MacPherson cut the connection, and for a long moment David just sat where he was, savoring the sweet taste of success. Then the system's connection alarm bleated again.

David ordered the system to pick up—and found himself confronting the annoyed face of Nick D'Aliso.

"The pay isn't that great," the hacker sneered. "So was it the great god technology, or just the challenge in general that got you to accept the job?"

"What's your problem with me, D'Aliso?" David asked. "You've been in my face—and, apparently, going behind my back—ever since I met you. Is my skin color an insult to your ethos? I thought that crap was over and done with."

D'Aliso's lips twitched in irritation. "Don't be a jerk."

"I know that having me around seems to blow your circuits," David said. "And I don't know why that would be—unless having me around worries you for some reason."

Nick D'Aliso stared hard at David. "You really don't get it, do you? Maybe you wouldn't, considering where you're coming from."

"Being a Net Force Explorer? A goody-goody?" David shot back.

Nicky da Weasel's eyes narrowed. "Yeah. It doesn't matter how much computer smarts you've got. We're talking business here." He paused for a second. "Dirty business."

"Have you got something to hide, Nicky?"

"The question is . . . do *you*?" D'Aliso was in full, stone-cold, Nicky-da-Weasel mode by now. "You're walking into a company a lot of people want a piece of. That means they'll all be looking at you, trying to find some kind of handle—some way to use you, to make you work for them."

He took a deep breath, trying to unfreeze his face. "I know what I'm talking about, David. I've seen it, played that game, made it my business." D'Aliso gave him a serious look. "And there are guys out there who could eat me for breakfast. It's not too late, David. You can still back out."

"And miss all the fun?" David asked.

Now D'Aliso got angry. "Look, jerk, I'm trying to do you a favor here—"

His voice broke off, and his body shifted so he was talking over his shoulder. "I'm jacked in to the Net, Sabotine. Give me a second."

David was instantly reminded of Mark Gridley at the Explorers meeting, getting distracted between veeyar and the real world. He looked down at Nicky da Weasel's shoulders. Yes, the hacker was wearing a Hardweare vest.

D'Aliso thrust his face forward, his expression mean. "You've been warned," he said. Then he cut out.

David sank back against his chair, but he was by no means relaxed. He was relieved that no one else had been in the house to hear what D'Aliso had said. It would have scared his little brothers, upset his mom, and angered his cop father.

Luddie MacPherson might reconsider the publicity value of an employee who could precipitate an investigation of Hardweare by the D.C. police.

There was something else there. . . . David took a deep breath, trying to still his emotions long enough to catch an elusive thought. Nick D'Aliso hadn't been talking to a cat when he got distracted. He'd been speaking to Sabotine MacPherson.

Well, that wasn't surprising, David thought. *He's living in the same house with Luddie and Sabotine.*

Then it finally hit him—the timing of Nicky da Weasel's call. *He knew that I'd accepted the job!*

How?

David remembered Luddie's parting words. "I'll tell Sabotine you're joining the team. She'll get in touch with you."

If Luddie had told Sabotine, Nick D'Aliso had sure found out what was going on from her pretty quickly. Either he was somehow bugging the girl's computer—supposedly impossible with Hardweare computers—

Or Sabotine was somehow in league with him.

David suddenly felt as if he were lost in a pitch-dark room, not sure if his next step would find the floor or send him falling twenty stories.

Nicky da Weasel's sign-off came back to him.

You've been warned.

6

David took in the group sitting around his virtual workspace. "Thanks for coming, guys. I need some advice."

It was his usual circle of friends from the Net Force Explorers.

"Dump her," advised Andy Moore, lounging in midair.

Matt Hunter stared at him in disbelief. "Why do you think I called this meeting about a girl?"

Andy shrugged. "What else would the super-brain need our advice on?"

Megan O'Malley rolled her eyes. "Moore, you are *sooo* disgusting!"

"You just realized that?" P. J. Farris asked.

Leif Anderson simply shook his head.

"You think I shouldn't dump her?" David inquired.

"I think you must be crazy to ask this collection of clowns for advice on anything," Leif replied.

"This is a business question, not a personal one," David said.

"Another job turndown?" Leif asked.

Now it was David's turn to shake his head. "A job I've accepted, with Hardweare."

Daniel Sanchez did a double-take. "You got the job?"

"Outrageous!" Caitlin Murray, generally known as Catie, enthused.

The virtual room was filled with his friends' cheering.

Leif, however, was a little less enthusiastic. "Who offered you the job?"

"Luddie MacPherson himself," David replied. "According to him, after all was said and done, my connection with Net Force is what convinced him to hire me. His company faces a lot of negative publicity—people are claiming that the leaks can be traced to the Hardweare vests."

"And nobody can really take them apart to come up with a definite answer." Matt Hunter caught on to the problem quickly.

"I'm surprised you'd let these people use you as a—a kind of shill," P. J. said.

"I'm going to be working on program coding," David spoke quickly. "With the understanding that if I see anything that's not kosher, I'm free to bring Net Force in."

"You'd be better off out of it," Leif said abruptly. "I haven't met Luddie MacPherson, but I've had a run-in with his father. That was enough to put me off the rest of the family forever."

"Sounds to me like you're going to extremes there, Leif," Megan said.

Leif glared. "I had this antitechnology nutcase try to fry my brains, messing with my implanted circuits. The guy's son has a rep for getting his own way—and making inconvenient facts disappear. I've had a firsthand taste of that, too. Everybody's told him he's a genius. Luddie may have hired David thinking he can keep him fooled."

Spreading his hands, Leif turned to his friend. "I think this job could turn into more trouble than anyone would want."

A younger voice piped up. "David, if you decide to pass on the job, could you recommend me?"

All eyes in the room went to Mark Gridley.

"Have you even been listening to what we've been saying, Squirt?" Andy demanded.

Mark shrugged. "This MacPherson guy may think he's a genius, but I'll bet you I'm smarter."

"No takers there," David said. "Besides, Hardweare has enough young geniuses running around."

David then went on to tell his friends about Nick D'Aliso and his warning.

Megan gave David a look. "Well? You told Luddie Whoozis you'd call in Net Force if you came across anything that seemed fishy. What are you waiting for?"

"And what am I going to tell Captain Winters?" David burst out. " 'I need Net Force help! A notorious hacker was mean to me!' "

Megan definitely did not agree. "What about this Weasel guy finding out so quickly that you'd been hired? Obviously, he's intercepting Sabotine's computer messages."

"I don't have any proof of that," David objected. "Sabotine could have passed along the information personally to Nicky da Weasel. And before you try to make that into a big conspiracy, passing that information could be as innocent as office gossip or corporate need-to-know. We don't know what his full job description at the company is. For all we know, he has a full right be in the loop on my hiring."

"Maybe," Leif said. "But D'Aliso's warning is right on. Battlin' Bob MacPherson told me that several corporate big boys are going to end up fighting over Hardweare. And MacPherson might be a nut, but he's the sort of nut who's right on target, too. Now Nicky da Weasel is saying the same thing." He shook his head. "David, I'd bail from that company if I were you."

"But you're not me." David tried to keep the dismay off his face as he turned to the rest of his Explorer friends. "What do you guys think?"

"Bail," Mark Gridley promptly said.

"You rat," Andy Moore accused. "You're just saying that because you're hoping to scoop up the job." Glancing at David, he said, "I'd say stick with it." He grinned. "But then, I happen to like trouble."

"I think you should stay, too," Matt Hunter was more serious as he cast his vote. "Unlike Andy, I don't think it will be fun. But I think someone should be keeping an eye on what happens at Hardweare, and you've got the perfect in.''

"Git out of there, pal," P. J. Farris advised. "There's too many wild cards in this hand. You don't know which way this will go, but I'm betting it will get ugly. There are easier ways of earning college money.''

"Spoken like a true politician's son," snorted Megan with a toss of her hair. "You've got to hang in there, David. Hardweare is taking computer technology in a whole new direction. If people intend to mess with it, Net Force has to know—the sooner, the better.''

"That family sounds messed up—and I ought to know. My family is messed up enough." Daniel frowned as he spoke. "Get involved in their quarrels, and you're just asking for trouble. I don't care what kind of opportunity it is—I'd get out.''

"It's a one-of-a-kind opportunity," Caitlin argued. "Years from now you'd kick yourself if you bailed—and you know it, Gray.''

David felt his lips quirk in a half-smile. "Four votes to stay, four to go. Looks like I end up with the tie-breaker." He took a deep breath. "I'm not going to quit. I've got a chance to do some interesting coding and fatten up my college fund at the same time. There's definitely some weird stuff swirling around Hardweare, but there's no way of telling if it's a case for Net Force.''

He spread his hands. "I'll tell you one thing, though. No way am I going into this blind. I'm going to get in touch with Captain Winters. Maybe he can help me pin down some of these rumors about Hardweare.''

When his friends finally disconnected, it was nearly time for supper. David heard knocking on the door.

"Are you done yet?" his younger brother James wanted to know. "I still have some homework to finish.''

"Just a couple more minutes," David said. He returned to the computer-link couch, went through the static snap-crackle-pop of tuning in, entered the Net, and gave Captain Winters's Net address.

He found himself in a virtual duplicate of the captain's office—with a virtual version of the captain sitting behind the desk.

"David!" Winters said. "What can I do for you?"

David felt unexpectedly tongue-tied. "I—uh—didn't think you'd be working so late," he said a little lamely.

"Time and tide—and paperwork—wait for no man," the captain replied with a grin. "These may be virtual files, but it still looks like paperwork to me."

The thought of a fighting man like the captain shuffling files just about floored David. "Somehow, I don't think of you doing that," he said. "It doesn't seem right."

"Oh, it's been worse. When I was still in the Marines, for example. There were requisition forms for everything from rations to ammunition, about a bazillion reports to file—" Winters's good humor failed him for a second. "And the less pleasant items, like writing to the next of kin for each casualty." He lightened up. "I haven't had to do that for any Net Force Explorers. You guys keep your noses clean, and I shouldn't ever have to write one of those letters again. That's a nice feeling."

"I didn't expect you to be in the office, sir," David said. "If you've got things to do, I won't bother you. You can shift me to the message facility, and I'll record—"

"David, a big part of my job is to act as liaison with the Net Force Explorers. Let's liaise." Winters scowled for a moment. "Is that a word? In any event, it beats being a glorified file clerk. What's on your mind?"

David explained about his job offer from Hardweare and, more haltingly, about the weird stuff he and Leif had encountered in connection with the company and the MacPhersons.

"I don't know about any laws being broken," David finished. "But before I take the job, I thought I should find out more about Hardweare."

"I can tell you a little, right off the top," Winters replied. "Luddie MacPherson is an almost prototypical young genius. Net Force has received complaints about killbots deleting media files on MacPherson's private life. But by the time we check into the complaints, Luddie seems to have paid the complainers off—at any rate, nobody has ever pressed charges. That's not a fact we like to advertise—no sense giving other people the same bright idea. With the kind of lawyers MacPherson has been able to hire, no one is likely to succeed in making any charges stick, even if they want to.''

Winters leaned back in his virtual swivel chair. ''Regarding Hardweare, well, we're interested in the company for obvious reasons.''

David nodded. ''I know the Gridleys are evaluating one of the vests.''

''I've seen an initial report,'' Winters said. ''MacPherson has incorporated some remarkable innovations into that little package. And he's managed to keep a proprietary hold over a lot of those innovations, in a business where open architecture is the norm.''

''I guess it helps that there's a circuit to fry the whole vest if you try to see what makes it tick,'' David said.

Winters looked sour. ''Another example of the paranoia of a young genius at work.''

''Luddie picked me personally because of my connection with Net Force,'' David said. ''He feels that hiring me will help give the company credibility, maybe shut up some of the people blaming Hardweare for some connection with the business leaks.''

This news didn't brighten Winters's outlook very much. ''The young genius takes on public relations. Are you worried about being used as a smokescreen?''

''Right now I'm more interested in the accusations about the vests being linked to the escaping secrets,'' David admitted. ''Has anyone made a formal complaint?''

''Not with Hardweare's lawyers ready to leap into action,'' Winters said. ''But Net Force has reasonable cause for suspicion—off the record. The executives in the companies that have been burned all regularly wore Hardweare vests.''

''But executives all over wear the stupid things,'' David pointed out. ''It's one of those corporate status things. I bet they all wore Rolex watches and carried Mont Blanc pens, too.''

Winters shrugged. ''But a Rolex or a Mont Blanc won't

hold quite as much data, and won't blow up if you try to open the case. Most big corporations like to believe they've got reasonably airtight security. Some of them even have it. And there is the fact that the leaks have become a hemorrhage since the vests got popular.''

"Who's making the accusations . . . off the record?'' David asked. "You told us about leaks hurting a soda company, a fast-food chain, and an investment bank. I'm interested in the bank. Could someone be trying to soften Hardweare up for a takeover attempt?''

"It's a possibility.'' Winters thought for a second. "There's a media conglomerate who was embarrassed over details of their Hollywood accounting being made public. They also have a big stake in the software business. The security people at the investment bank were pretty bitter over the vests' privacy features. They've gotten burned by maverick executives before.''

He glanced at David. "One thing that strikes me is the company that *hasn't* complained about anything.''

David leaned in. "And what company is that?''

"The Forward Group.''

David sat up a little straighter. "Those are supposed to be some pretty bad guys.''

"The new superpower, if you believe the news magazines. An international conglomerate that conducts its own foreign policy, bringing down governments that don't please them and installing more convenient rulers.''

David nodded. "They supposedly helped to bankroll the junta that took over Corteguay—although that deal didn't turn out the way they expected. The new government threw out all foreign companies.'' He frowned. "The Forward Group started as a high-tech company—''

"I actually knew Jeffrey Forward, the guy who founded the operation,'' Winters said. "He was a real visionary. But when he died, the sharks took over the company.''

"They do have a predatory reputation,'' David said slowly. "But it's all rumor and innuendo—like what's being done to Hardweare.''

Winters looked grim. "It's not all rumor. Top executives

of companies that got in Forward's way have suffered convenient . . . accidents.''

David tried to read the captain's face. "But you haven't
heard anything about Hardweare being targeted.''

''Hey, we might not hear anything, considering what the
Forward Group spends on security. Countries could run their
whole intelligence agencies on that budget.'' He paused. ''Or,
for that matter, their armies.''

''Or maybe their security is so good, they haven't had any
leaks,'' David suggested. ''That would let Hardweare off the
hook.''

''I haven't seen anything,'' Winters objected. ''But then,
whoever is spreading these leaks is sort of . . . haphazard.
Sometimes items appear in newsgroups where people might
be interested. And you know newsgroups. Some are legit,
some are wacko. Sometimes information is sent to the media.
In that case, we might not hear any accusations. Forward has
lawyers, too.''

''And killbots, I imagine,'' David said cynically.

''A few items have been forwarded to law enforcement tip
lines,'' Winters finished. ''All I can say is that they haven't
heard anything, either.''

The captain paused for a moment. ''Yet.''

David spent an uncomfortable, sleepless night, wondering if
he was doing the right thing. The next day after school,
though, he faced decision time. Sabotine MacPherson called.

Her hologram image looked a little harried. ''Sorry to do
this to you, David. I was hoping to give you an easy project
to bring you up to speed. Instead, we've got a bit of a crisis.
The guy who was supposed to be working on this just quit.''

She shook her head. ''Young geniuses, you know.''

The upshot was that she'd send a limo to pick him up so
he could get the necessary files and a briefing. ''It's a long
ride and short notice, I know,'' Sabotine apologized. ''But
until you have the software installed on your end to make a
secure link, we can't send stuff over the Net.''

David laughed. ''Including the software that would allow
us to make a secure link.''

"Anyway, I'm sending the car now." Sabotine glanced at her watch, and didn't look happy. "I'm supposed to be going out at five—this is going to be tight—"

She sighed. "Just get here as soon as possible, okay?"

Sabotine's request simply couldn't be kept in D.C. rush-hour traffic. Even though—thanks to the Net, telecommuting, and onboard computer guidance systems—the snarls bore no resemblance to the legendary traffic jams of the late twentieth and early twenty-first centuries, nobody was doing over twenty miles an hour. As the limo crawled along the Beltway, David fumed and fretted in the backseat.

Great impression I'm making, he thought gloomily. *Could Sabotine simply be setting me up to fail?*

It was well after five o'clock by the time they reached the country road that led to the MacPherson estate. David had asked the limo driver to call ahead when they'd first gotten stuck. Sabotine had said she'd try to hold on as long as possible to give him the packet personally. But if they were much later, the materials would be awaiting him at the guardhouse, and the briefing would have to wait until he'd installed the security programs on his home computer.

David leaned forward in his seat, as if he were pushing the limo to greater speed by his own mind power. There was the fieldstone wall—

A disgusted sigh seeped out of him. And there was a limousine, leaving the front gate.

There were two people in the backseat—Sabotine and Nick D'Aliso. Both were dressed up.

Were they going out somewhere? David wondered. *Have I been rushing like a maniac so I wouldn't mess up their date?*

His thoughts were interrupted when an old Dodge came whipping around the corner, aiming straight for the leaving limo. David's driver swerved wildly as the Dodge cut in, blocking the other limo's path.

A big, craggy-faced man got out of the car. "Sabotine!" he shouted. "You won't take my calls, but you're going to speak to me anyway. I'm your father."

Battlin' Bob MacPherson approached the passenger com-

partment of the limousine, a pleading expression on his face.
But that changed when he saw who was with Sabotine.

"You *scum!*" roared the big man, ramming a hamlike fist
at the window. "I told you to stay away from my daughter!"

7

The limo with David aboard jolted to a stop, and the driver got out, pulling a heavy automatic pistol from a holster under his jacket. Sabotine's chauffeur was doing the same thing. Both men's guns covered the big man who claimed to be Sabotine MacPherson's father.

Battlin' Bob MacPherson, if that was who it was, might be strong, but even he couldn't smash his way through the bulletproof glass of an armored limousine. He was doing his best, though, single-mindedly pounding on the window next to Nick D'Aliso.

Sabotine's driver had his pistol in a two-handed grip, aiming for Battlin' Bob's chest. "Stand away from the car, pal. *Now.*" His voice was pure cop. David ought to know. His father was a homicide detective. This was the tone of voice Dad used when things got deadly.

The big, craggy-faced man wasn't taking the guy seriously, however. He continued pounding his fist against the armor-glass window.

"We *will* shoot you if you keep this up," the other driver growled. He'd moved to a spot where he could still get a shot at the big man, even if Battlin' Bob tried ducking for cover behind the car. Considering the ex-wrestler's size, David wasn't at all surprised that neither bodyguard wanted to try taking him down physically.

Sabotine MacPherson came stumbling out of the rear door on her side of the limo. Tears streaked her face. "Daddy, stop! *Stop it!*"

The driver blanched as the body he was supposed to be guarding blundered into his line of fire. "Ms. MacPherson! Get back!" he called desperately.

Sabotine looked as if she wanted to run into her father's arms, but she stayed on her side of the car, and Battlin' Bob stayed on his.

The big man had no choice in the matter. A squad of armed guards came charging out of the mansion gates, followed by a scowling Luddie MacPherson. Watching the two confront each other, David could detect some points of resemblance between them. Luddie had inherited his father's big build, and he had a softened version of the older MacPherson's craggy features.

Right now, however, his face looked more like a thundercloud—his eyes flashed with repressed lightning. "The court gave us an order of protection against you," he snarled. "You aren't supposed to come within half a mile of this estate."

"You and your lawyers may be able to bamboozle a judge!" Battlin' Bob shouted back. "You sure paid generously enough to have them steal my daughter from me. But you and your high-priced legal talent are dead wrong if you think a piece of paper will keep me away from Sabotine!"

"I didn't expect the court order to stop you," Luddie coolly responded. "That's one of the reasons I hired these guys— and their guns."

He stared at his father as if he were examining some sort of dangerous—and very ugly—bug. "It's a shame you didn't actually come inside the gates. Then we could have shot you down as a trespasser."

Battlin' Bob opened his mouth to respond in kind, but was cut off by a wail from Sabotine. "Both of you! Just—just stop it!"

The girl's beauty had never seemed more fragile as she

looked back and forth between her father and her brother. Sabotine looked as if she were caught in the buffeting winds of a storm, torn one way, then the other. Tears flowed unheeded down her cheeks. "How many years has it been since the two of you could sit in the same room without sniping at one another?"

Her accusation came out as a series of gusts. "I thought—whatever else—the court thing settled the whole mess. But now you"—she thrust an angry finger at Battlin' Bob—"come storming up, ready for a new battle. And you"—she whirled on Luddie—"you're ready to *shoot* him!"

"Honey," the elder MacPherson said.

"Sabotine," began Luddie.

"I'm sick of it, do you hear? *Sick of it!*" Sabotine yelled. "The two of you treat me like the prize in some weird game of keep-away. Well, you can play without me. I'm out of here!"

She grabbed the chauffeur's arm. "Get in and drive," she ordered.

The man looked at Luddie, but got no guidance there. Sabotine's brother was staring at the ground.

Battlin' Bob stood with his big hands outstretched, looking oddly helpless as Sabotine's limo backed up and swung around his Dodge. Seconds later the big car rounded a corner and disappeared. David and the others could see that Sabotine never once looked back through the rear windshield. But Nick D'Aliso put an arm around her shoulders.

The older MacPherson whipped round to glare at his son. "Did you see that?" he demanded. "You took her away from me, locked her in your fortress here . . . and she ends up with Nicky da Weasel." He spat. "Weasel, hell! The man is a human rat!"

Luddie himself didn't look too happy at this turn of events. But before he could answer, the distant wail of a siren came to them across the Virginia countryside.

"Oh, yes, we called the cops," Luddie said, reverting to his earlier coldness. "Why don't you just get out of here—spare your glorious cause the cost of your bail money?"

Battlin' Bob MacPherson turned on his heel and got behind

the wheel of the old Dodge. It roared off down the road, away from the gate—and from the oncoming sirens.

Luddie turned to one of the uniformed guards. "When the police get here, apologize—say we handled the problem ourselves." His shoulders slumped. "It's almost true."

Then he gestured to David's driver. "Get that thing inside the gates before the local law takes you for the intruder we reported and starts shooting."

David lost sight of the young inventor as the driver brought the limo inside the wall of the estate. The gates swung shut behind them.

Then Luddie appeared from inside the stone guard station set beside the gate. He carried a small package in one hand, going over the contents. "Datascrips," he said, handing it to David. "Sabotine labeled each of them. Install our communications security protocol and look over the one marked 'Background' if you want. Sabotine will get in touch with you—um—"

"When she gets back?" David suggested.

Luddie glanced at him with a flash of his usual humor. "I was going to say 'when she cools off.' " He sighed. "Well, at least now you know why I try to keep my family under wraps."

As abruptly as he'd left after David's interview, Luddie turned and began heading back to the house.

David sat in the limo, waiting until the police were finished at the main gate. Then the driver turned the limo around and brought him home.

Leif Anderson laughed at the perplexed-looking hologram image of his friend. "That's some story, David," he said, leaning back in front of the holo pickup. "But, since I don't think you're setting up your own gossip newsgroup, I guess you must have some reason for telling me all of this."

"No." David gave him an annoyed look. "I thought you'd just like the opportunity to tell me 'I told you so.' "

"Ooh! Good one!!" Leif responded, pretending to clutch at his heart. "But seriously, what can I do for you?"

"You can help me sort it out!" David shook his head as if

it hurt. "I feel as though I've gotten caught in some HoloNet soap opera. Business intrigue, dysfunctional families, forbidden romance—"

"Oh, I see," Leif interrupted him. "You're looking for me to explain the strange ways of the rich folk." He glanced up at the ceiling, then turned his eyes straight to David. "Most of them are just like the rest of us—only more so. Especially when they're not happy. They've got the bucks to act out— or act up—when the rest of the world would just have to sit there and take it."

"The people I saw today were totally out of control," David said.

He got only a shrug in reply. "You can almost expect that from nouveau-riche types—the ones who've just made their money. Big bucks seem to go right to their heads. My parents are exceptions, but there aren't many." Leif gave David a crooked smile. "I ought to know—I'm nouveau riche myself."

"And what's Battlin' Bob's excuse? He's hardly swimming in dough," David pointed out. "Or is he used to criminal activities thanks to working for the Manual Minority?"

"*Some* people connected with the Manual Minority have been accused—and convicted—of terrorist activities," Leif said tonelessly. "Spokesmen for the movement always refer to these as quote—'the actions of extremist splinter factions'— unquote."

"Sounds good, but not convincing," David said.

Leif's answering grin was lopsided. "On the other hand, Battlin' Bob's police record isn't notable for cyber-terrorism— usually he got nailed for stopping speeches to come down and punch hecklers in the head."

"You should have seen the way he was punching the window on that limo." Reliving the moment made David shudder. "Nick D'Aliso is lucky that was bulletproof glass. Old Mr. MacPherson looked ready to kill him."

"How would you feel if you saw a girl you liked in the backseat of a car, going out with Nicky da Weasel? Multiply that by about 130, and you'll begin to approach how a father might react to his daughter being in that position." Leif grimaced. "I've been on the receiving end of that sort of emotion from a few parents myself."

David grinned. "A total overreaction to your reputation."

Leif gestured helplessly. "In most cases, yes."

David's smile dimmed. "Did any of them try to kill you?"

After a brief silence Leif finally said, "It never got that far."

"Do you think—" David began, stopped, then tried again. "Do you think this whole leak problem could stem from something . . . personal?"

Leif blinked at the sudden shift in the conversation. "I don't see—"

"Suppose someone wanted to trash Hardweare. They leak a whole load of business secrets. And who gets the blame? The computer that's every executive's favorite fashion accessory."

"And this someone would be?" Leif prompted.

"Battlin' Bob MacPherson." David rushed on to make his case. "He's got the means—he and his people are willing to use technology to advance their cause. You know that?"

Leif winced at the reminder of the attack on his implant circuits. "Yeah, I noticed."

"And he's got motive. For an antitech agitator, what could be worse than a son who turns out to be a computer genius?"

"A son who divorces his family—and then goes to court to steal his sister away, too." Leif shook his head, denying his own words. "You're right. This *is* too much like a HoloNet soaper," he scoffed. "I was seeing it more as a spy drama."

They laughed, dismissing David's theory—at least for now. David cut the connection, and Leif was alone in his room, looking at a dead holo display.

He was bored! His folks were still keeping him on restricted Net access after his misadventure at *The Washington Post*. Leif restlessly paced around his room. The movement helped, but not enough. Maybe it was time to run off some steam. He put on sweats and a pair of running shoes and went down the hall to the huge parlor where his parents entertained. His mom sat on a couch, watching a hologram dance recital. She'd chosen this room because she could see the dancers life-size.

"May I go out for a while?" Leif asked in a pause between dance movements.

His mom gave him a considering glance. She must have decided he couldn't get in much trouble in the outside world, because she gave her permission.

After taking the elevator down from his parents' penthouse apartment, he crossed the lobby to the doorway facing Park Avenue. Taking a deep lungful of New York air, Leif waved to the doorman standing in front of his building and set off down the street. What next? He had no particular plan. He could walk to the gym. Or maybe he'd head over to Central Park and do the loop there. It didn't matter. The run was just an excuse to get him away from the house. Leif felt as if he had just escaped from prison. He was happy simply to be out on the sidewalk.

Then he realized someone was walking beside him, keeping pace. Leif glanced over and felt a chill run down his spine. He recognized the man matching him step for step. He'd met him before under difficult circumstances and had assumed he would never see him again.

The man's name was Slobodan Cetnik, and he was a spy— or at least a secret policeman—in a Balkan dictatorship called the Carpathian Alliance. The Balkan peninsula remained one of the world's worst trouble spots—for hundreds of years the home of deadly fanatics who fought bloody wars. The losers of the last round of fighting represented just about every ugly -ism of the twentieth century. The Carpathian Alliance was a pariah state, currently existing under a punishing technology embargo.

Cetnik had been part of a plot to circumvent those restrictions, getting at American technology by way of Hollywood. A large holo-studio producing a big science-fiction series had run a contest for teen viewers, letting the worldwide audience design racing vessels for what the series had called "The Great Race." The prize had been a treasure trove of computer gadgetry, items which would allow the Carpathian alliance to make up a lot of technological ground.

Cetnik had chaperoned the C.A. team, the power behind the

curtain, so to speak, determined to win even if it took lying, cheating . . . or killing.

David, Leif, Andy, and Matt—all of them Net Force Explorers—had entered the race, won it, and defeated the Alliance's ploy. Cetnik had returned to his country in disgrace. So what was he doing here now?

Leif could see some differences in the man. The Cetnik he remembered had been sleek like a hunting cat. Today, he looked stressed, shabby—more like a junkyard dog. But still very dangerous indeed.

"I shouldn't be here," Cetnik said conversationally. "I'm supposed to be in Washington, with a delegation that's speaking to one of your more soft-headed senators. Even to get there, I had to call in every favor I ever earned. Since my failure in California, I am . . . not in a good position."

His dark eyes seared Leif with their hate. "But I had to risk everything when I encountered a certain name in a report discussing possible American security leaks. Your friend David Gray is working for Hardweare, and we believe those wearable computers somehow allow individuals to tap corporate secrets. We wish him to find out how it's done—and turn the information over to us."

"You can wish for anything you want," Leif told the agent, "but why would David do that for you?"

Cetnik shrugged. "He might do it for *you,*" he said silkily. "And you might do it for . . . Ludmila Plavusa."

8

Ludmila Plavusa's name was the last thing Leif expected to hear. She was a girl—a hacker from the Carpathian Alliance—Leif had met in Hollywood. She'd been helping her team win the Great Race by charming information out of competing racers. But when people started getting hurt, she'd helped the Explorers stop Cetnik and his helpers.

Leif remembered her fondly. It didn't hurt that she was blond and gorgeous.

"What about Ludmila?" Leif asked through suddenly dry lips.

"I was just thinking," Cetnik said. "What a shame it would be if bad things were to happen to Ludmila and her mother—just because *you* were uncooperative."

Leif glared. "You dare, you bas—"

Cetnik interrupted. "Yes, rich man's son. Me. Bad things have been happening to *me* since I returned to the homeland. Your meddling cost my government a major intelligence resource."

Cetnik's plot to win the contest had gotten help from a very strange source—a new political party, the anarcho-libertarians. Driving mainstream politicians and corporate types crazy, they

attacked what they called "the government rules monopoly."
They combined an insistence on social freedom—driver's li-
censes at age sixteen—with a terrifying sense of social responsibility. Drivers who got into accidents paid heavily. As
the political flavor of the month, the anarcho-libertarians gen-
erated a lot of interest. But they lost Leif when it came to their
cockeyed view of the past. They idolized certain history-
makers, calling them "avatars" for imposing their personal
wills on the march of events. Unfortunately, many of these
avatars were, in Leif's opinion, ruthless dictators and mass
murderers.

This perverse viewpoint on history led some people to see
the Carpathian Alliance, a nation shunned by all decent countries, as some sort of heroic "go-it-alone" state. Well, the
Alliance wasn't stupid. They manipulated these dupes for the
obvious benefit—collecting hard currency through a variety of
front organizations. But C.A. intelligence agencies took advantage of the anarcho-libertarians in other ways—wringing
out aid, money, and information for their spies.

Unfortunately, this cozy arrangement had blown wide open
when a radical Hollywood offshoot of the anarcho-libertarian
movement went too far trying to fix the Great Race for their
C.A. heroes. Repercussions were still shaking out, which was
probably why the Alliance delegation was lobbying Congress,
no doubt complaining about some unfairness or other.

Oh, yeah, Leif thought. He'd felt it was reasonably safe for
Ludmila to return home to the Carpathian Alliance. Cetnik
couldn't go after her without admitting just how badly he'd
screwed up his mission. But Leif had never considered that
Cetnik might use Ludmila as a lever to force *him* to do favors
for the C.A.

"I don't expect an answer right now," the C.A. agent was
saying as if Leif were suddenly his new best friend. "You
should take a couple of days to consider the . . . possibilities."
Cetnik then slipped right into business mode. "I'll expect a
call from you by the end of the weekend." He handed Leif a
slip of paper. "This is the hotel where I can be reached. You
can be Igor Lachavsky, inquiring after your cousin Ludmila.

I'm sure I don't have to warn you to use a public Net connection.''

Leif said nothing. Not using an easily traced Net connection was a basic precaution in making prank calls—or, Leif suddenly realized, in espionage.

Even so, Cetnik was taking a chance. The C.A. delegation had to be drawing some attention from counterintelligence agencies. Playing a lone hand had some disadvantages for Cetnik.

If only Leif could think of some way of turning that to his own advantage! But his brain remained stubbornly numb as Cetnik ended their little meeting.

''I expect I'll be hearing from you.'' The C.A. agent smiled, but there was a chilling kind of certainty in his voice. It was the tone a fisherman might use when he was sure the hook was well and truly caught in his quarry's gut.

Leif wasn't sure whether Cetnik stayed around a little longer, enjoying what he'd done, or if the agent walked off quickly. He himself spent the next hour running along the Central Park loop almost blindly, his pace hurried, as if he could somehow outrun the lump of cold dread weighing on his heart.

Ludmila . . . Leif remembered his annoyance—actually his jealousy—when he saw her flirting with guys from the other teams, even though Leif knew it probably meant disaster for their racing efforts. He remembered her face as Cetnik had screamed at her after she'd saved Leif's life, along with all his teammates. He remembered her smile as she relaxed with him and let the real Ludmila come out. Exhausted after a worried, sleepless night, she'd dozed off against his shoulder. But most of all, Leif recalled Ludmila's patient, almost sad tone as she described her day-to-day life in a fanatical dictatorship. It wasn't terrible; people weren't out of their minds with fear. It was just that they always had to be . . . careful. In a million small ways they had to watch what they did and said.

She never told him what happened if someone made a mistake in that wary dance around the edge of the volcano. But Leif could imagine. And he could imagine what Ludmila and her mother would go through if Cetnik made good on his

threat. The girl had lost her father years ago in the last out-
break of war in that troubled part of the world.

Leif shuddered. He knew he wasn't a coward. For the thrill
of it, he'd tackled tough ski runs, runs that regularly broke
arms and legs; he'd crashed parties that were supposedly un-
crashable; he'd even spent some time in the cockpit taking the
controls of a friend's private plane. He also knew that there
was something in him that enjoyed twisting rules until they
were just about—though not quite—broken.

Right now those two parts of Leif were savagely fighting it
out. One side wanted to tell Cetnik to screw off, to stop him,
to hurt him if necessary. But doing that would put Ludmila in
danger. One word from Cetnik, and the machinery would start.
And the C.A. had very a horrible efficiency at grinding people
up for the good of the State.

Go along with him, Leif's sly side urged. *String the guy
along. Knowing David, he probably will find out whether—or
how—secrets leak from people who wear Hardweare vests.
You might be able to get Cetnik off your back.*

No. If he gave in, he'd never get Cetnik off his back. Leif
knew he'd become . . . what had Cetnik called it? An "intelligence resource." If he went along with what Cetnik wanted,
the C.A. spy would then have *two* levers to pry future treason
out of him.

And if he didn't . . .

Leif could see Ludmila's laughing face in front of him as
she briefly relaxed her guard. Then he remembered the expression of sick fear on those perfect features as she begged
him to hide her from her keeper—Slobodan Cetnik.

Leif Anderson ran on, his body hunched a little as if someone had punched him in the gut, his hands jammed in his
pockets. It was an impossible choice. Whichever way he went,
the consequences were . . . unthinkable.

Think, he commanded his usually agile brain as mile after
mile passed beneath his feet. *You can always concoct schemes
and scams. Come up with a solution for this problem!*

But he couldn't engineer a way out of this difficulty by
himself—and who could he ask for help? Mom and Dad loved
him, but Leif doubted they'd understand how he'd gotten in-

volved with Ludmila, much less why he felt the need to protect her.

David knew about Ludmila and even liked her. But Leif couldn't drag his friend into this mess. For one thing, it would be like asking David to make up his mind for him. More important, it would leave them both trapped in Cetnik's web.

That's what this C.A. creep wants, Leif suddenly realized. Ludmila was the lever that worked on Leif, who'd be the key for David, who'd give away the secrets of Hardweare—and then permanently be available to have his brains picked.

This was blackmail, extortion . . . and espionage, plain and simple. Leif knew the person he *should* be taking this problem to—Captain Winters. Net Force was supposed to take on people who attempted computer spying.

But Leif couldn't go there for help, either. He might trust the captain, but Winters wouldn't be put in charge of this case. Whichever agent got the job would be interested in nailing Cetnik—not helping Ludmila.

Leif found himself walking across a grassy field in Central Park, not quite sure how he got there. *Come on, come on!* he urged his increasingly confused brain.

But every time he thought he had a halfway decent scheme, he ended up picking holes in it. He even managed to come up with drawbacks in schemes he'd already discarded. For instance, if he went to Winters, how could Leif be sure that Cetnik wouldn't learn who'd double-crossed him?

If only I could make it too dangerous for Cetnik to mess around with Hardweare—without him being able to blame me, Leif thought. He stopped in his tracks as a glimmer of an idea hit him.

Leif began retracing his steps across the grass, moving almost at a run. *I might be able to pull this off,* he thought, *but I need to make the call from home. This isn't a job for a foil-pack phone. I'll need every advantage I can get—watching facial expressions and reactions in detail. That means using my holo-system back home.*

Soon enough, Leif was sitting back in his room, facing the holo pickup of his system. He debated going into veeyar to make this call, but decided he needed the indefinable feel of reality, not to mention the lack of distraction from that first painful entry into the Net. He almost barked instructions at the computer, then sat waiting for the connection to go through, holding his breath. Was it too late? Would he still be in his office? Would he pick up?

Struggling to keep a calm expression, Leif let go a long sigh of relief as Captain James Winters appeared in the display over the computer.

The captain looked rather skeptical when he saw Leif.

"Well, Mr. Anderson, this is a surprise. What can I do for you?"

"You make it sound like there's always something I want." Leif let a note of complaint creep into his voice.

"Perhaps that's because whenever I talk with you, you end up playing me like a violin," the suspicious Winters replied.

"*I* don't want anything," Leif told him. "I'm worried about David." One thing he had to give to Winters. The captain was quick on the uptake.

"The Hardweare business?"

Leif nodded. "I think David's told you a little about the company and that three-ring circus of a family."

Winters gave a short, sharp laugh. "I think that's a generous description of the MacPhersons."

"Well, the circus now has an animal act," Leif said. "Battlin' Bob MacPherson caught his daughter in the same car with Nicky da Weasel—excuse me, Nick D'Aliso. And Daddy simply went ape."

"I didn't hear about this." Winter now leaned forward over his desk.

"David was wondering out loud if there was some connection between the family's problems and the whispering campaign against Hardweare. I'm wondering if there's something more," Leif said. "Nick D'Aliso tried to warn him off from taking a job with Hardweare. At the time, we thought he was trying to get rid of a potential competitor. Now that I've had time to think about it, I'm not so sure. Maybe he knew more than he was telling."

"And maybe it's time to rattle a few cages and see what we hear," Winters said.

Leif nodded, afraid to trust his voice. He'd just gotten exactly what he'd wanted.

"Whoever it is, make it brief," David's mother said when the call came into the Gray house. "Dinner's almost ready."

David answered at the living room system.

"Captain Winters!" he said in surprise.

The captain looked somewhat ill at ease. "I'm torn in two directions," he said abruptly. "You know how I warned all the Net Force Explorers about getting too involved in this leak problem we've encountered."

David nodded. "We're just to pass along any interesting information, so we won't get killed."

"Well, it's beginning to look as if you've put yourself right in the middle of the case," Winters said. "We decided to take a look at Hardweare—and at the principals involved with the company. A couple of hours ago one of our agents came across what may be a serious development. He spotted Nick D'Aliso entering the headquarters of the Forward Group."

9

David tried to exert some control on the blizzard of thoughts flying through his head. "Has D'Aliso done any work for the Forward Group before?"

"They've got a corporate policy against freelance hackers—except in their dirty-tricks department." Winters shook his head. "Jeff Forward is probably spinning in his grave. The guy was a young genius, like your new friend Luddie Mac-Pherson. Forward started out as a hacker and held on to that mind-set all his life."

The captain smiled in recollection. "You know, he did everything he could to stop Net Force from being set up. Called us the Cyber-Thought Police. His idea was, if anybody misbehaved on the Net, some hackers would get together and flame the offending sites out of existence." Winters laughed at David's expression. "He called it ultimate freedom of information—the kind of benevolent anarchism idealized by the hackers from the 1980s."

"He doesn't sound like the kind of guy who'd set up a monolithic corporation as his memorial," David said.

"That wasn't Forward's idea. He didn't like companies. That's why it's the Forward *Group*. It was originally just an ad-hoc alliance of hackers whose specialties interlocked. They took on projects that single hackers couldn't handle alone. The jobs kept getting bigger and bigger until Forward had to take on partners and be more businesslike. Even then, he used to drive the bean-counters crazy because of the jobs he *wouldn't* take. Forward had high-tech answers to any problem—but he refused to handle military contracts.''

"So what happened to make the Forward Group what it is today?"

"Forward died. The business types took over. Forced the specialists into suits and a proper corporate existence. Purged the hackers who wouldn't fit in.''

"And probably drove most of the creativity right out of the company," David said.

Winters nodded. "But they learned to raid schools, catch the talent young and try to indoctrinate the best and brightest—or lure them with big bucks. They appropriated creative companies, either buying them up or stealing their ideas and intimidating them into silence.''

"Could they be trying that with Hardweare?" David asked.

"From what we can tell, most of their security budget— and a surprising amount supposedly for 'research'—goes into corporate espionage," Winters said. "With a flood of secrets gushing into the Net and being blamed on Hardweare, who could tell if some were quietly going to the Forward Group?"

"David!" His mother's voice brought him back from the shadowy world of corporate skullduggery to more everyday concerns—like supper.

Winters must have heard the call, too. "I'll let you go to your mom," he said. "Just bear in mind, whatever Net Force does with Hardweare and Forward, I don't want you investigating."

"But you said it yourself," David put in. "If I find information . . ."

Winters had that "torn in two directions" look again. "Yeah. I'm sure it wouldn't be rejected. But personally, I'd be happier if you got out of there."

• • •

David was so distracted through dinner that his brothers began making fun of him. "I said, 'Pass the potatoes,' Mr. Space-o." Tommy giggled.

Mom scolded the eight-year-old, but David noticed that she looked a little worried. He made an effort to take a bit more interest in what was going on around him, but it wasn't easy. All sorts of questions kept popping into his head, things he wished he had asked Captain Winters.

Was there hard proof that the Forward Group was using Luddie MacPherson's invention as some sort of espionage vacuum to suck up corporate secrets? What was Nick D'Aliso's involvement? Was he an information conduit to Forward? Had he somehow programmed the leak into the supposedly tamperproof computer vests?

But one question above all really disturbed David. What was Nicky da Weasel doing at the offices of the Forward Group? The obvious answer would be he was working for them . . . as a corporate spy. But an undercover agent would have lots of ways—inconspicuous ways—to pass along information other than walking in the front door.

Nick D'Aliso must know how to bounce messages all over the Net. He could infiltrate inactive Net sites to use as data drops—in fact, given Nicky da Weasel's talents, he'd be able to mess around and program *active* sites to take his messages.

So why was he strolling into the corporate gates of the Forward Group, where he could be spotted? Where he *had* been spotted?

Did the Forward Group think it was so well-insulated from whatever was happening at Hardweare that no connection could be made?

Maybe it was just a case of big-business arrogance. These guys had pretty much had things their own way—buying up companies, strong-arming competitors, changing foreign governments to suit themselves. Of course, this time, they were up against the U.S. government. David felt a sudden chill. Unless, with their spies and their assassins, they thought they'd reached the point where they could win here.

•   •   •

Slobodan Cetnik strolled down the hall of his Washington hotel. But his seemingly easy stride hid a careful, nervous search for hidden watchers. From the moment he stepped into the lobby downstairs, he'd paid special attention to anyone who seemed to be loitering, sitting, reading the paper . . . keeping an eye on new arrivals. Had he seen these people before?

Then, on the way upstairs, he'd checked out the hotel workers—bellmen, porters, cleaning staff on the floor. Were there faces here he *hadn't* seen before?

Those were the easiest ways to infiltrate people into a hotel for surveillance duties. Cetnik had used both approaches himself at various points in his career.

As he approached the door to his room, however, his shoulders relaxed a little bit. He'd been confident no one was tailing him when he set off on his private business, but he'd taken all the usual precautions just to be sure. He was certain he hadn't been followed to New York.

And as far as he could see, no counterintelligence agents seemed to be awaiting his return.

It was just another example of soft, decadent, gadget-happy American life. The lawmakers his delegation visited had been surprised at the thought of hosting actual meetings instead of computerized get-togethers in veeyar. When Cetnik had left, he'd taken a train up to New York, paying with actual American dollars so there would be no record of the transaction. Then he'd walked the couple of miles from the station to the home of Leif Anderson. And now, twelve hours later, he was back, with no one the wiser.

In the homeland he'd have faced identity checks if he tried to leave a major city or enter another one, for trying to ride on major transport, and at least one police demand for an internal passport from any obvious stranger on a city street.

There, I'd have been helpless to move around and develop my plans, Cetnik thought. But here, the *Americans* are helpless, useless . . . what was the word they always used? Clueless!

Cetnik slipped his digitized card-key into the slot in the door and pushed it open. He was three steps inside before he realized he wasn't alone in the room.

"What—?" The C.A. agent flicked his wrist, and the ceramic knife which was invisible to X-ray scans dropped into his hand. Even as he stabbed out, however, the aerosol spray was going into his lungs, his eyes, soaking into his skin—

The man in the dark suit became grotesquely large, then impossibly small, as if Cetnik were seeing him through a distorted camera lens. The knife dropped from Cetnik's suddenly leaden fingers. Something strange was happening to the floor. It seemed to be tilting wildly to his right.

Cetnik flung out an arm, attempting to balance himself. He tried to call out for help, but his voice emerged only as a thin whine.

The floor treacherously swung to the other direction, and Cetnik suddenly found himself falling.

His arms and legs seemed somehow disconnected from his brain, but he could feel his heart pounding in his chest from rage and terror.

The man in the dark suit bent over him. Cetnik saw a perfectly bland face, a face so ordinary no one would remember it.

Except, of course, that the face was gray. No, the world was going gray. Cetnik blinked, then couldn't seem to get his eyelids open.

Everything went black.

Leif Anderson sat silently in his room, going over his conversation with Captain Winters for about the hundredth time. He didn't think he'd given too much away. The captain had gotten into the habit of wariness when Leif called, certain that some sort of con job was underway.

But there was no possible way that Winters could uncover Leif's real motives for this last call. His concern for David was real enough, even if it wasn't the overriding reason why he'd warned the captain about the new troubles at Hardweare. Maybe Winters would think the spoiled playboy had turned over a new leaf.

Leif didn't care what anybody in Net Force thought, as long as they made the environment around David Gray too hot for any foreign spy to come near. Maybe the captain had gone all the way, telling David to pull out of Hardweare before things really got nasty.

That would be the best all around, Leif told himself. *David would be annoyed if he found out that I sicced Winters on him—*

Leif scratched out that thought. *Nobody can know what I did,* he told himself. *There can't even be a whisper about it. If Cetnik suspected I was responsible, he'd make Ludmila's life a living hell.*

He took a deep breath, trying to calm his suddenly racing heart. *I've never felt like this,* he thought, sick with misery. *I can't even think straight because of this never-ending, unrelenting fear. . . .*

He glanced longingly at his computer setup, especially at the holo pickup. Maybe he should make a call to David, see what was going on. Had Winters talked to him yet? David had called Leif for advice when this whole thing started.

Maybe I should offer to advise him now, Leif thought. *I'll tell him to get out of there, beg him if I have to.*

Just as quickly, he turned away. He'd have to be crazy to try that. For all he knew, Cetnik could have a tap on his communication lines. More likely, he—and maybe a lot of other people—were listening in to David's voice and data traffic.

No, Leif told himself grimly, *I'll just have to sit here and sweat it out until David calls me with any information. And then I'll have to sound shocked and surprised, not just for David, but for anybody else who's tapped into the line.*

He allowed himself a long, slow smile. *I hope Cetnik is listening in. It will help convince him I had nothing to do with it.*

Unless . . . what if Winters mentions my call to David? What if David calls me to let me have it if he loses his job?

Then all his effort would be for nothing. Ludmila and her mother would suffer the worst vengeance Cetnik could come up with.

Like a mouse on one of those little exercise wheels, Leif's mind went back to his conversation with Captain Winters. *Could I have told the captain to keep my name out of it?*

Not without making the already suspicious Winters really

start digging into why you were calling, another part of Leif's mind cynically answered.

Leif realized he was rocking back and forth in his seat.

I'll make it up to you, he mentally promised David. *Dad must have some kind of job you could do. He's still a little mad at me over what happened at the* Post, *but who knows? Having me go to bat for you might surprise him enough to clinch the job. He'll think I've gotten less self-absorbed.* He pushed away the personal thought. *I don't care what Dad thinks. Just don't call up complaining that I lost you your job. Not for me. For Ludmila.*

When the system gave off the tone for a holophone connection, Leif's overstrained nerves nearly sent him flying from his chair.

He didn't even bother with voice commands, stabbing at buttons with his fingers. Leif's gut tightened when he saw David's face in the display.

"We've got stuff really cookin' tonight," David said abruptly. "Winters decided to bring Net Force into the Hardweare thing, and guess who was spotted making up to the Forward Group? Nicky da Weasel!"

David's surprise news made it easier for Leif to hide his relief that his plan had worked. The captain obviously hadn't mentioned who had put the idea of digging deeper into Hardweare into his head.

But David wasn't finished with the evening's surprises. "My dad called with some weird news, too. I almost wonder if it's connected, somehow. Remember that C.A. spy we came across in Hollywood? He was in Washington for some reason. I guess we'll never know why. Anyway, he took a twelve-story tumble out of his hotel room window. The manager called the cops, and the case was turned over to the homicide squad. Dad's looking into it as a suspicious death—probably murder."

10

Leif couldn't believe what he was hearing. Words sputtered from his lips. "What . . . How?"

David looked at him in concern. "What's the problem, pal? I know you didn't like the guy. He nearly got us killed out on the West Coast. So why are you getting so broken up to hear he's been erased from the Great Datascrip of Life?"

"You're sure it's Cetnik?" Leif demanded.

"Not at first," David admitted. "The guy was traveling under a phony passport and registered in the hotel under that name. When the manager called the police, the other people in the C.A. delegation played dumb—'Ve know noddink!' "

Leif winced at the corny accent.

"Dad said some of the embassy people looked scared to be dealing with the police," David went on.

"Probably equating the D.C. cops with the stormtroopers back home." Leif's voice was harsh. "How did your dad get Cetnik's true identity?"

"Fingerprints," David said. "It's standard procedure to take prints at a possible crime scene. Federal computers spit up Cetnik's name and record." He smiled grimly. "Prints and photos are two of the most effective weapons against spies.

When the Net Force agents took Cetnik into custody after the Great Race thing blew up, they got both.''

David looked a little sick. "Since Dad knew that I knew the guy, he showed me a photo of the deceased. It was Cetnik, even though he didn't look too good.''

David stared at Leif. "What's going on with you?''

Leif's eyes were shut as he sank back in his seat. "He was working this alone.'' The words gusted out like a sigh. "She's safe.''

"Who's safe?'' David wanted to know. "Who's alone?''

"Ludmila Plavusa and Slobodan Cetnik, respectively,'' Leif replied. "I'll tell you everything.''

He explained about being accosted by Cetnik in New York. Then he went on to describe the agent's seemingly unbeatable extortion scheme. Leif didn't actually use the words *heartless* or *fiendish*, but David got the point.

"What a scum-sucking dog,'' he said briefly.

"Yeah. But he had his teeth in my leg, and it was obvious he wasn't going to let go.''

"You should have come to me,'' David complained. "Or better yet, gone to Captain Winters.''

"What could either of you have done?'' Leif demanded. "Cetnik would just have gotten his claws into you. Or, if Winters stepped in, Cetnik might have been neutralized—but we couldn't be sure about Ludmila.''

"Unless Cetnik was dead,'' David agreed. They both stared at each other in total silence.

"Hey, I *know* I didn't do it,'' Leif insisted. "And it couldn't have been Net Force. That's just not the way they operate. If agents had gotten on to Cetnik, they might have arrested him—that's what I was afraid would happen. But this isn't the Carpathian Alliance. Inconvenient people don't simply drop dead on command.''

"Unless they get in the way of the Forward Group,'' David suddenly said.

Again, the two boys' eyes met. But they didn't say a word. A shudder went through Leif's body, as if a blast of cold air had invaded his usually comfortable room.

Finally Leif sighed. "Do you want to call Winters?" he asked. "Or should I?"

"Maybe you should arrange a joint connection," David suggested, "so we can both talk to him at once."

Captain Winters was still at his office. His hands turned to fists on top of his desk as he listened to what David and Leif had to tell him.

"Well, isn't this nice," the captain said sarcastically. David could see the effort he put into unclenching his fingers and laying his hands flat on his blotter. "I guess I should thank you for the early warning, David, although I'd probably have gotten a report sooner or later."

David nodded. "Dad said the feds would definitely be moving in on a case involving the death of a foreign agent."

Winters turned to Leif. "As for you, Anderson, I don't quite know what you thought you were doing. Have you been reading old *Spyboy* comics and decided to be a superhero? Knowing your background, I can't believe you let yourself be put in that position—"

"I didn't *let* myself be put anywhere," Leif protested. "Cetnik confronted me with an impossible set of choices. If I tried to do anything, someone would be hurt."

"You allowed him to put the squeeze on you, to control your options—and your thinking. From the sound of it, you weren't even thinking, just reacting emotionally. That let Cetnik take control."

"I did the best I could when I talked to you." Leif's voice sounded helpless. "If Cetnik saw Net Force agents swarming around Hardweare—and David—he'd have to give it up. As long as he couldn't blame it on me, nobody would get hurt."

"But somebody *did* get hurt," Winters pointed out. "Cetnik was murdered."

"It could have been an accident," Leif tried to argue, but his voice sounded weak.

"Or Cetnik could have suddenly become convinced he could fly," the captain said coldly. "Spies rarely die natural deaths . . . especially when they're operating undercover in an enemy country. That's what the U.S. of A. is to the Carpathian Alliance.''

Leif went pale. "You can't be saying—"

"No, this wasn't a sanction, hit, liquidation, or whatever catchy phrase the spy novelists are using nowadays."

"Deletion," David blurted out unthinkingly. He quickly shut up, almost shriveling under the glare Winters directed at him.

"Mr. Cetnik was not deleted—at least, not by agents of the U.S. government," Captain Winters assured them.

And he ought to know, David thought.

"But we're obviously not the only players in this game," the captain went on. "Before you told us about our late foreign visitor, we had no idea of any C.A. involvement in this situation. There may be other national governments with an interest—not to mention terrorist groups or companies."

The captain's face went completely stony. "What worries me is the timing of this killing. Somebody—some person or persons unknown—eliminated a competitor for a potential bonanza of information leaks presently associated with Hardweare and its wearable computers."

He paused for a second, then said, "If I sound like a lawyer, that's because the existence of this supposed treasure trove of data hasn't been proved—it's just rumor, extrapolated from a few leaks which have appeared on the Net."

Like David, however, Leif had seen past the legalese. His face, already pasty after Winters's scathing words, went gray. "You think Cetnik got killed *because* of me—because I maneuvered Net Force into taking a harder look around Hardweare." He swallowed loudly—more like a gulp, David thought. "Whoever killed Cetnik did it now, before investigators found him." Leif looked even more sick. "And to do that, they had to know that Net Force would be looking. Which means either they tapped into my call, or your office . . . or they've got a mole somewhere in Net Force."

Winters responded with the barest of nods. "Whatever the killers meant to do, they've just upped the odds drastically. We'll be looking into the Hardweare matter as a possible national security breach instead of a corporate nuisance." He sighed. "I wouldn't want to say anyone's death had a good side, but that is a benefit. Then, too, Cetnik's removal gets *you* out of the fire."

The captain stabbed a holographic finger at Leif. Then he turned worried eyes to David. "I can't say you're in too deep—at least, not yet. But I'm not easy in my mind about you working for Hardweare."

"I'm not even out there," David protested. "All I do is work to scrunch down their coding and leave the occasional E-mail."

"Even so, Cetnik saw you as the magic key to open the information floodgates," Winters pointed out.

David shook his head. "From the looks of it, they should be after Nicky da Weasel instead." He hesitated for a moment. "How much can I tell the folks at Hardweare about all this?"

"You can tell them everything," Winters replied. "Their lawyers know most of it, anyway. They're currently stone-walling federal warrants. Net Force has already begun its investigation."

Shortly afterward, David found himself in another three-way conversation. But this time his listeners were together in the same room—the luxurious parlor of the MacPherson mansion. Luddie sat on—or in—the self-adjusting couch. Sabotine had chosen a wooden stool that had been hand-carved into a work of art. Brother and sister stared out of the holo display at a diffident David Gray.

"When I took the job, I warned you that I'd tell Net Force if I came across anything that merited their attention. Well, I feel that should work the other way, if possible, and I've gotten Net Force approval for this. You know they're investigating Hardweare in connection with this wholesale leak problem."

Luddie nodded. "My lawyers have been busy, demanding that the government show cause. At the worst, the lawyers tell me, we might have to give a couple of depositions."

"It *will* be worse than that," David told him. "This has become a national security case. A foreign agent was found dead in what can only be called suspicious circumstances. He was trying to put the screws to a friend of mine, to force me to find the supposed Hardweare access to people's secrets.''

"Suspicious circumstances," Sabotine said slowly. "You mean this person was . . . murdered?"

"I never really believed it would go this far." Luddie struggled off the sofa and began pacing back and forth. "In any kind of communication, there's a varying ratio of garbage to information." His face twisted. "Nowadays, the Hardweare name has so much garbage plastered to it, we're drawing flies. Does Net Force know where this spy came from?"

"The Carpathian Alliance," David said.

"Those idiots barely *have* computers!" Luddie burst out. "Of course they'd believe this—this crap that's being spread about us!"

"The government is saying things that are just as crazy," Sabotine spoke up. "They're saying that Nick D'Aliso is working for the Forward Group."

"I don't know if they'd go that far without more investigation," David said. "But I was told Nick was spotted going into the Forward offices."

"That makes no sense!" Sabotine burst out.

Luddie nodded, his face grim. "Of all people, Nick should know that these rumors about getting stuff through our vests are all bull. Hey, I hired him initially to check security—and he wasn't able to break into Hardweare! He's the best, and he found the vests were uncrackable."

He stalked back and forth, talking to himself as much as to David and Sabotine. "This whole thing is an attempt to force us to open up the system architecture on the vests so some Mexican manufacturer can make them cheaper, or some corporate colossus like Forward can switch around a couple of doohickeys and break my patent. Those scumballs specialize in that, you know."

Luddie stopped and took up a defiant pose, the heavy muscles in his shoulders straining the seams of his jacket. "Well, it's a free country—my competitors can give it a try. And Nick D'Aliso is especially at liberty to play it any way he wants. If he wants to suck up to Forward, he doesn't need a job here." He turned to his sister. "I'll tell the guards he's no longer welcome here. Sabotine, revoke his access codes—including any personal ones. Arrange for someone to pack up whatever nonbusiness stuff he has in his room—we'll ship it wherever he wants."

Sabotine stared at her brother as if she'd been slapped. "Luddie—" she began in a trembling voice.

Luddie MacPherson may have been in the same room with his sister, but they might as well have been on distant mountaintops. "I didn't say anything about how you two spent your time together," Luddie said, though David could see Luddie hadn't been happy about it.

"That was personal, but this is business. If Hardweare fails, everything we've got here"—his gesture took in the elegant salon with its one-of-a-kind artworks—"is gone. Until we get this straightened out, I can't trust Nick D'Aliso—and I can't trust having him around you."

"You never liked Nick," Sabotine raged. "I think *you're* listening more to the garbage than the information when it comes to him!" She stormed out of pickup range—probably to the other side of the mansion, David thought.

Luddie turned to David, a big, capable-looking guy with a helpless expression on his face that soon changed to disgust and embarrassment. "I don't know why you're so lucky, David," he said. "But you somehow always manage to catch us at our best." He glanced off after Sabotine. "Almost as good as a HoloNet soap, and no commercials."

And all the bedroom scenes have taken place offstage, David thought, but he kept his mouth shut.

"There's also more boring stuff, like real life," Luddie went on. "I've been following your progress at compacting the code on our programming. The work you've done has been nice and tight. You should expect a new download, probably this evening."

David was a little surprised. "There's a bet I wouldn't have won," he said. "I figured after this conversation, I'd be finished at Hardweare."

Luddie shook his head. "For being honest? I wish all of our people were like you."

He didn't say any more, but David could hear Luddie's thought as clearly as an echo. *Especially Nick D'Aliso.*

Later that evening David sat in his virtual workshop. He'd finished with the last of the coding still on hand from Hardweare, and went to check for downloads. Had the promised programs from Hardweare appeared yet?

David checked his virtual in-box and sighed—empty.

Then he squinted. No, there was something in there. He'd been expecting to see a big, clunky, makeshift program icon—who wasted time and energy crafting an icon for a work in progress?

Instead, this icon was tiny, a miracle of miniaturization, a work of art. For some reason David was reminded of Sabotine MacPherson.

Maybe this is what Hardweare's finished products look like, he thought. *This is Sabotine's taste exactly—except a bit on the morbid side.*

The icon was a tiny gravestone, made up of even tinier human bones. Probably some sort of horror sim for bored executives.

David picked up the icon, intending to run it through his disassembler, then go to work on the naked code.

Instead, the workshop around him shifted, becoming a bleak, garbage-strewn alleyway.

David scowled. *Great,* he thought. *The stupid program's gone and activated itself.* But he had to admit he was curious.

"Run simulation," he called out. At first nothing happened—then he began running down the dark alley.

David tried to take over his veeyar character. But nothing he did moved the action from an apparently preprogrammed track. He had absolutely no control over the simulation. *How do you work this thing?* He shouted the usual computer commands. None of them had any effect. He just kept running, his lungs starting to burn, panic struggling to take over his brain.

He recognized the sensation—it was just like the sudden onslaught of terror he'd felt when he'd dropped from the clouds in Luddie MacPherson's introductory sim.

Nick D'Aliso said he'd been working to introduce intense emotional triggers into Hardweare's entertainment programs, David suddenly recalled. Was this another example of Nick's work?

Was it just coincidence that Hardweare downloaded a D'Aliso program for me to work on? Or is this some sort of hacker's revenge?

That wasn't a welcome thought. Stirring up his own very real fears made the programmed panic attack all the stronger. David was dashing forward wildly, stumbling over abandoned garbage bags and loose trash. Something squished wetly under his left foot as he came up to a wooden fence that was taller than he was. Flakes of paint clung to the warped boards. Years ago someone had painted a mural.

"Willie-Boy died here," the faded letters announced.

Even as he scrambled over the fence, fighting the mindless rush of adrenaline, a part of David had to admire the craftsmanship that went into creating this simulation. He got a splinter from one of the crumbling boards.

What David really wanted to do was look back at whatever was pursuing him. But the program wouldn't allow that. He swung over the top of the fence, fell almost full-length on the pavement on the other side, scrambled up, and resumed his mad run.

Something darted across his path—either a small cat or a huge rat—and David stumbled again.

That's when he noticed the bright-red dot that appeared on the brick wall beside his head.

That was the trademark of a laser gunsight. David lurched away, all rational thought temporarily swamped by a new rush of terror. Was this supposed to be a horror sim?

He got a few more steps in, dodging from side to side, then something slammed into his shoulder, and terrible pain rolled over him.

I've been shot! David realized. *But this is VR! I know I keep my pain thresholds set lower than most people, but I shouldn't be able to feel this much pain! The safety protocols in my computer—*

He was down on his face among the sour-smelling garbage

on the stained concrete. What felt like a red-hot spike being driven through one shoulder had rendered his right arm useless. His left arm was moving, though. His fingernails clawed at the pavement; his legs pumped as he tried to scrabble a few inches forward.

David couldn't seem to catch his breath. His muscles weren't quite working right. He couldn't even push himself up. All he could do was make spastic little attempts at crawling as footsteps came closer and closer from behind him.

Sobbing moans erupted from David's lips. He wanted to turn his head, to look up and face his pursuer, but the program wouldn't allow him to. He lay with his face pressed to the cold concrete as a hot metal ring—the barrel of a recently fired gun—was pressed to the back of his neck.

Then the system crashed.

David was in his bedroom, half-twisted across the computer-link couch. It was as if his body had actually responded in reality to the frantic commands to turn around that David had issued in that upsetting little sim.

He was in an uncomfortable position, but he didn't shift—he was afraid to trust his trembling muscles. The adrenaline overload from the sim, it seemed, created real world consequences. That was the worst computer crash he'd ever gone through. Besides the usual headache a crash left behind, his mouth was as dry as baled cotton and his stomach felt as if it were trying to crawl out of him. He kept gulping mouthfuls of saliva, trying to keep from throwing up. Every muscle he had seemed to be quivering with exhaustion, his heart was racing, and his right shoulder hurt—a sort of phantom echo of pain related to the gunshot wound he'd experienced in veeyar. Very strange.

David finally got his breathing under control. Whatever juices Nick D'Aliso's subliminal cues had turned on, they were very, very potent. He was still shaking with fear.

This kind of sim could give people heart attacks, David thought. How could D'Aliso expect to market this to a bunch of pampered executives? He must have taken at least one very long step past the safety blocks of regular virtual reality to get the effects he'd achieved.

David knew a lot about the safety restrictions programmed into the world of veeyar. When he created a sim, especially a space-related one, he expected people—including himself—to behave intelligently. Lapses of attention in space could have fatal consequences, so David programmed a certain amount of pain to result if people screwed up. Those signals could, of course, be overridden by anyone going into the sim. Settings for the degree of stimulation allowed or desired could be calibrated in every VR system. Users could adjust those settings to reflect their own personal tolerances, from avoiding all pain entirely to playing macho and risking the allowable maximum. It was a matter of user's choice. David's friends usually trusted him enough to let his settings stand when they entered his sims. They knew him well. They were making an informed choice.

But I had no choice in what happened to me, David thought. *It's as if my body was somebody else's puppet, going through a set of programmed motions. Nick D'Aliso's a crackerjack programmer. This is hardly typical of Nick's work, which usually features dizzying numbers of choices. This sim was strictly linear, with the user stuck as it played out, a prisoner of the predetermined events. Which wasn't to say the sim was simple, without artistry.*

Remembering the incredibly real details, David examined his hands. One palm seemed inflamed—the place where he'd gotten stabbed by a splinter scrambling over that fence.

Details real enough to leave stigmata—and a one-dimensional action line. It didn't make sense.

Unless it was a sim designed so the viewer couldn't escape—a sort of nasty farewell present from Nicky da Weasel himself. David shuddered again. Maybe he should count himself lucky that the system had crashed when it did. He only wished his Net safety features had activated a little sooner. Admittedly, he tended to keep them adjusted to allow the maximum level of sensation, but this was ridiculous.

David shakily got to his feet, ordering the computer to shut down. He wobbled a little as the holo display turned itself off. He'd check out that little program again later—*much* later, and from the outside.

His hand suddenly clapped to his mouth, and he dashed for the bathroom.

Right now he had more immediate concerns.

The next morning was Saturday. David stayed in bed as long as his younger brothers would let him. As he blearily headed down the hall to wash up, his mother asked, "Feeling better, dear?"

David considered for a second. It seemed as though a night's sleep had let him shake off the worst effects of his veeyar adventure. "Guess so," he said. "I don't know what came over me." No way was he going to admit that a computer program had attacked him.

Speaking of which—David quickly showered away the last traces of cobwebs and headache, then quickly headed back to the bedroom. The little guys were out in the living room, watching the Saturday morning holos on the big system out there. David turned on his computer, running it strictly with spoken orders. No way was he reentering veeyar until he knew what awaited him there. He ran some diagnostics, just a check in case D'Aliso's sim had acted as a Trojan horse for worse surprises, then called up his directories.

He frowned as he looked at the holo display. There was no trace of last night's download. Apparently it had been erased in the crash that had ended his computing session the evening before. David called up memory utilities, trying to see if any traces remained in his virtual in-box. No joy. Maybe if he'd tried this stuff right after the crash—

David shook his head. No. He'd been too busy barfing his guts up back then. Programming simply hadn't been possible.

He frowned. Well, if he didn't have the copy, he'd just have to check in with Hardweare and get another one.

Or find out where it came from if Hardweare didn't send it, a cynical little voice in the back of his mind pointed out.

• • •

Sabotine MacPherson's holo image looked a little surprised to see him when he called in. "I've finished with the last of your previous batch," David told her. "That's being uploaded to you as we speak."

Usually, he'd just upload and leave an E-mail. But David had a question to ask, and he wanted an immediate answer if possible. "Now what do you want me to do with the game or whatever you downloaded last night? It looks pretty buggy to me."

"What game?" Sabotine asked. "I was just about to send you an E-mail. The stuff Luddie wanted to zip your way won't be moving until tomorrow at the earliest." She gave him a crooked smile. "This investigation has got things turned completely upside down."

"So you didn't download *anything*?" David pressed. "I got a program, with what looked to be Hardweare protocols."

Although, he had to admit, he hadn't really paid much attention when he picked up the icon.

"I didn't send it, and I'm pretty sure Luddie didn't, either. He's been spending all his time with our lawyers." Sabotine looked at him curiously. "What was it?"

"A very nasty little sim that self-started, ran me through the wringer, and then blew the system," David said grimly. "Hacker's work."

Sabotine looked shocked. "You're saying Nicky—"

"Well, he certainly didn't like me as much as he liked you," David said. "It wouldn't help his feelings for me to have Luddie fire him right after talking with me. Maybe he felt I deserved a lovely parting gift."

"That's not like Nicky at all!" Sabotine protested. "I'd like to see this program."

"So would I," David admitted. "But it got erased—or erased itself—when my computer crashed."

"So you don't actually have it," Sabotine said.

"And I don't have many people who would send me something like that," David pointed out.

"There's nothing I can tell you one way or the other. I haven't spoken to Nicky since Luddie cut him loose." She looked pretty upset. "But the guy I know wouldn't—"

Sabotine hesitated a moment, and David could imagine what she'd been about to say—something about Nicky not wasting his time on petty revenge.

Instead, she finished with "He wouldn't do something like that."

David thanked her and cut the connection. *The guy you know was on his best behavior, taking you out,* he thought. *Dropping a little sim-bomb on someone who'd gotten on his bad side sounds just like the Nicky da Weasel I've always heard about.*

The hologram bleeped again, and David made the connection, expecting to see Sabotine calling with something she'd forgotten to tell him.

Instead, he found Leif Anderson looking out at him with a serious expression. "You free to make a veeyar visit in a little bit?"

"You make it sound like we're going to court," David joked.

Leif didn't laugh. "In a way we are. I've got to explain what's been going on to my folks. And I'd rather have one of my more reliable, respectable friends on hand to help with the job."

David was about to come up with some sort of polite refusal when he saw the pleading look in Leif's eyes. "Okay," he said with a sigh. "I can try."

His visit took place in the virtual equivalent of the Andersons' living room. It wasn't as large, as high-tech, or as filled with art as the MacPhersons' parlor, but it was no doubt a very expensive room.

I guess that's what happens when you've got interior decorators, servants, and no younger brothers always jumping on the couch, David thought.

Mr. and Mrs. Anderson were very polite, greeting David, seating him in a chair that felt much more comfortable than it looked, then turning to their son.

"A couple of things have happened that I think you should know about," Leif began. As he spoke, David could see that the Andersons knew a little about Hardweare and the leaks on the Net. But they were shocked to hear about Cetnik's extortion attempt and his death.

"Maybe it's a terrible thing to say, but I'm glad that man is dead," Mrs. Anderson said.

Leif's father had pain in his eyes as he looked at his son. "If you'd come to us—"

Leif looked just as unhappy. "I couldn't tell you, just as I couldn't tell David." He turned to his friend to verify what he said. "Otherwise, an innocent person—a person I liked—would suffer. And I would be responsible."

Magnus Anderson sighed. "Heaven knows, we've talked enough to you about responsibility. I thought that when you got involved with the Net Force Explorers, that might have a good effect." The older Anderson glanced at David, who caught his meaning. *Nice, steady, dependable kids to act as role models.*

"Instead, we find people trying to kill you through veeyar, and spies threatening you and your friends." Leif's father shook his head. "And I thought *I* led an exciting life!"

David found himself speaking up. "But Leif is being responsible, Mr. Anderson. He's telling you all this stuff—and taking responsibility for it."

"After the fact," Mrs. Anderson pointed out.

"I know you mean well, David," Mr. Anderson said. "And you, too, son. I don't know what we'd have said if you'd come to us. We definitely have a problem here, and I'm not sure how to resolve it."

Leif braced his shoulders and turned to David. "Thanks for helping me explain things," he said.

David nodded. Obviously it was time for him to go. Things would probably get very personal from this point on. Leif's father had been very cool, very calm. Not at all like David's dad, who'd have probably hit the roof, bounced off it, and laid down the law on the return trip.

Cutting the veeyar connection, David found himself back in the cluttered bedroom he shared with his brothers. Even through the closed door, he could hear them playing one of their crazy games, running up and down the hall.

Leif had big bucks, a beautiful apartment with his own private suite, and parents out of one of those sophisticated, very civilized European holo-dramas.

So why do I feel sorry for him? David wondered.

He went outside to join his family. The Saturday morning computer-animated kid shows were coming to an end. Robo-Mouse was kicking some serious ArmorCat butt. Heroes and villains looked like real animals, except that no real animal David had ever seen was ever quite that cute, or had such big eyes.

Cheered on by Tommy and James—David's younger brothers—Robo-Mouse had ArmorCat by the tail and was swinging him overhead with a whizzing sound. The mouse let go, and the cat plowed through several skyscrapers with plenty of crashes and booms.

Some things never change, David thought. *Growing up, I've seen this same toon with several different characters and cruder computer graphics. But the story never changes.*

The episode came to its usual end, and the kids rushed over to their father, their faces eager. "Are you coming outside with us, Daddy?"

"We're gonna play!"

Martin Gray was only too glad to spend his day off being a daddy instead of a homicide detective. David's mom smiled fondly as the boys led their father off, each holding one of their father's hands.

"Do you want me to turn this off?" David gestured toward the holo display.

"No, I'm just going to change the channel," his mother replied. "We can still catch some of the noon news."

She shifted the display to the holo-news channel, where a pair of plastic-looking anchorpeople with perfect hair smiled out at the audience.

I'm surprised they've never used computer animation to replace these types, David thought as the newspeople shared a loud laugh over a lame joke. *They're human versions of Robo-Mouse and ArmorCat, with more perfect hair than normal people—and bigger eyes.*

The anchorman looked into the holo pickup, his big smile switching to an especially pretentious expression. "Thanks,

Leslie-Anne,'' he said, his voice zooming down to hit the low notes.

Okay, we get it, David thought in disgust. *Serious news ahead.*

It could be anything from the death of a popular star to the latest scare news about the disease of the month. But a familiar logo appeared behind the anchorman, reading ''Crime in the Streets.''

''With the ever-improving crime statistics in the D.C. area, violent death comes as more of a shock,'' the anchorman intoned. ''We had a suspicious death yesterday . . . and today, an out-and-out case of *murder*. Jay-Jay McGuffin reports.''

The scene shifted to a blow-dried anchor-in-training standing against a brick wall wearing a totally unnecessary trench coat.

Except it makes him look like a Holo-Net detective, David thought. *I wonder if they poll viewers to see what they expect the newspeople to look like?*

Jay-Jay was busy trying to make somebody's run down these skeevy backstreets sound like *The Odyssey.* ''Perhaps,'' he said dramatically, ''the still-unidentified victim might have successfully made his escape, except he chose to run down this alley—''

The camera followed the newsman down a garbage-strewn alleyway. David felt a cold prickle run down his back at the reminder of last night's unpleasant sim.

''An alley blocked by this reminder of a long-forgotten gang murder.'' Jay-Jay went on in his most pompous tones, but David wasn't hearing.

He was staring in horror at an eight-foot-tall wall of weather-beaten wooden boards, where ancient flakes of paint clung like scabs on an old wound.

The mural was even more faded in full daylight, but David could read the letters painted under the almost-obliterated picture.

Willie-Boy died here.

This was the same site as last night's nightmare sim!

12

Spinning on his heel, David sprinted from the holo-display as if his clothes were on fire. He dived through the door to his room, barking orders to his computer.

"Net search. News items, all major media sources, regarding murders, mysterious deaths, bodies discovered in the Washington, D.C., area within the last . . . twelve hours," he finally decided.

"Processing," the computer responded.

David paced up and down the room, waiting for the computer to retrieve and organize the requested data. "Computer, collate all items," he ordered. "Most recent to be projected first."

Years ago he'd have been confronted with an avalanche of murder data. But Washington, like many big cities, had become a considerably more peaceful place these days. David liked to think that his father, and men like him, had a lot to do with that. David only had to sort through a few references to other cases before he found the information he sought.

There wasn't much of it. The body of a young male—no ID, his pockets turned out—had been found in a decayed backwater section here in Washington. With the neighborhood scheduled for demolition and rehabilitation, the area had been virtually deserted.

Police had responded to calls about the shooting and found the body. Checking out the area, they'd come across a place where someone had been camping in a ruined building. According to the report, it didn't sound like a homeless person living rough. Cops discovered a sleeping bag, supplies of food and water, and a laptop computer with heavily encoded files.

A search of the usual fingerprint files showed that the deceased hadn't had a police record—and offered no hope of quickly identifying him. The coded computer and Washington location suggested a foreign connection to some—could the dead man have been a spy?

David's thoughts immediately swung to Slobodan Cetnik. Could this somehow be connected to him?

Ridiculous, a nervous voice insisted from the back of his mind. *This has nothing to do with you.*

Except that I saw that alley last night, David thought. *I ran down it and was shot. . . .*

He wished he could dismiss the nightmare images skittering around his brain as just a bad dream. Could he have imagined the download, the whole tormenting episode of the chase? Could he have dozed off on his computer-link couch?

Or could someone have somehow recorded and downloaded the dead man's last moments? There was the crash . . . and the feeling in his gut when he'd seen the image of the wall across the alley.

David read on to find a quote from one of the cops who'd found the hideaway. "It was a good enough place to live, for a rathole. The guy had even managed to hack the electric company and get power."

Hack. Encoded computer. The dead man was a hacker.

A sick churning began again in David's gut. He turned off the computer and headed back to the living room. "I have to go out for a little while, Mom," he said. "Gotta talk to Dad."

He went downstairs and out of the apartment building, setting off for the neighborhood park. Sure enough, there was Martin Gray, playing catch with James and Tommy. The game was *not* preparation for a career in the major leagues. In fact, it looked like more of a chance for the younger guys to run back and forth yelling, "To me, Dad!" "No! To me, Daddy!"

Instead, Dad lofted a high blooper in David's direction. David snagged it on the fly, then walked over to hand it to his father. "Dad, do you have a minute? We have to talk."

Martin Gray took the ball and tossed it to James. "You guys take over for a minute—*gently!*"

Then he turned to his oldest son. "What's up, David?"

"While you were working last night—" David stopped and tried a new approach. "There was a piece on the news today about a body found in an alley somewhere in the Southeast section. Were you in on it?"

"Not my case," Dad replied. "Why?"

"I may have a possible ID." David took a deep breath. "I think it may be Nick D'Aliso."

Martin Gray's eyebrows rose in surprise. "That guy you were working with at Hardweare?" He thought for a moment, then shook his head. "You said he had some run-ins with the law. We checked fingerprints. His should have been on file."

David nodded. "I read about that. But, Dad, D'Aliso was a hacker. Given enough incentive, he would have been able to weasel into federal records and change the files."

A new chill ran down his back as an unwelcome thought entered his mind.

Or somebody else might have futzed up the records to hide the identity of a dead Nicky da Weasel.

Dad dug out his wallet and began tapping numbers onto the foilpack keypad, first switching it to telephone mode, then giving it the phone number. "Hey, Des. Marty Gray here. Anything new on that execution-style killing in the alley? Uh-hmmm. Still no ID? I heard a name you ought to run down. Nick—I guess Nicholas—D'Aliso." He spelled it out. "Sure, I'll hold."

David stood beside his father, wondering if he'd wandered into some strange twilight zone. Here they stood, talking about a murder. In the background his kid brothers were running, giggling, having the time of their lives.

His father stood holding the line, alternating between looks of "If you made me give up my day off for nothing . . ." with glances that said "Please don't be right."

"I'm still here," he said abruptly. He straightened slightly. With every word he heard, Martin Gray became more and more a cop.

He put his hand over the foilpack and turned to David. "The fingerprints in D'Aliso's file *are* different from the ones on the body. But with a name to go on, they can call up the dental records as well—and those matched perfectly." He turned his attention back to the phone.

"Des, I have to talk some more to my source about this—no, I'll get back to you—soon."

He cut the connection, glanced to where Tommy and James were trying to see who could bounce the ball harder, then faced David again. "You know, son, most dads would find it flattering to have a son interested in their business." David's father sighed. "But I can't say I'm happy to see you getting involved in *mine*."

David nodded, equally unhappy to have any sort of connection to a homicide.

Martin Gray's gaze grew harder. David had seen the look before. "Cop's eyes," his dad called it.

"When you told me, you knew I'd have to ask. How did you know it was D'Aliso?"

"I didn't," David said. "At least, I hoped it wasn't." He went through the whole explanation, the self-loading download, the weird chase sequence, the murder, and the system crash.

"There's no trace of the file's icon on the computer now," he finished. "I looked this morning. Then, on the news, I saw the same place from my—I was about to say my nightmare. But it was real, wasn't it? And when I heard about the murder victim who seemed to be a hacker—well, I had to come to you."

Martin Gray shook his head. "If it weren't my son telling me this, I'd be—very, very doubtful," he said.

David thought for a moment. "Does anyone have an idea when D'Aliso was killed?"

His father went back to his wallet-phone and hit redial.

"Des, I have one more thing to check, then I'll head down to see you. Do we have a time of death?" He listened, then turned to David. "Somebody dialed 911—a 'shots fired' call—a couple of minutes before ten."

David nodded. "Let's go check my computer. Even if we can't check the download, we can certainly trace the crash and reboot times."

Dad gathered in the younger boys, and they all headed back to the apartment building. Mom stiffened a little when she saw the look on her husband's face. She took Tommy and James into the kitchen for a snack without asking what was going on. David and his father went down the hall. A couple of orders settled the question. According to the computer's internal records, the crash took place at 9:57.

"We'll have to go downtown," Dad said.

A couple of hours later David still sat in an interrogation room, going over his story with several of Dad's colleagues.

Des O'Connor, the detective in charge of the case, shook his head as they entered the information into a file server. "I guess I'd have to call that story . . . pretty screwy, and I'm restraining myself out of respect for your dad. We've checked what we can. Public utility transmission records do show a Net transmission to your house at the time in question."

The detective gave David a speculative glance. "Obviously, you weren't physically present at the murder scene. We've got your mom and both brothers as witnesses to that. They all saw you burst out of your room and heard you redecorate your toilet with everything you had for dinner, just after this D'Aliso character got his. It would be nice to know who sent you the download, but it was done on a completely bogus account. Maybe if we can get into D'Aliso's computers without causing a meltdown, we'll get an answer to that little mystery."

O'Connor was obviously not thrilled with David's story, which wasn't a surprise. Cops are great fans of Occam's Razor, the scientific principle that says the least complicated theory which fit the facts is most likely to be correct. For O'Connor, that eliminated things like ESP or an out-of-body experience—or a phantom download—to explain David's knowledge.

If David hadn't experienced the download, he'd be skeptical, too.

Detective O'Connor shrugged yet again. "As things stand now, you've only told your father and us about this download. Please keep it that way. No statements to the press or going on the HoloNews to give interviews. We want to hold back your story—and any mention that we've identified the body as D'Aliso."

"I understand," David said. From his father, he'd learned certain tactics the cops used. Keeping details out of the media helped to determine whether witnesses were giving truthful testimony.

David noticed another measuring stare from O'Connor. There was another reason to keep some facts as a reality check—it helped deter cranks from making fantasy contributions. It also kept the real perpetrator guessing how close the police actually were to solving the case.

"Is there anything else you're holding back at this point? Stuff I might know because of the download and shouldn't talk about?" David asked.

"Nothing you can help us with," O'Connor replied. "Just a common-sense kind of thing. The dead guy—D'Aliso—was wearing a Hardweare vest under a sweater." The detective shrugged. "The place he was hiding out was a cesspit—abandoned buildings, some of the streetlights gone. On those dark streets he'd stand out like a lit Christmas tree if he didn't cover the thing up."

O'Connor gave David a crooked smile. "And it ain't the kind of neighborhood where you'd advertise owning a comb, much less an expensive computer toy."

Leif Anderson sat in his room reading a book—an actual, turn-the-pages type book, no holotext, hypertext, musical accompaniment, or sound effects. Well, he did have the system in his room playing some background music. Otherwise, he might as well have been a hundred years in the past. So far, he'd come to the conclusion that the good old days must have been a lot quieter.

He was still leading a somewhat restricted life, although things had gotten a bit better after he and his folks had talked things out. Leif was also making an effort not to get involved in anything that would strain the family peace right now.

Then David's call came.

Leif could see his friend was upset before David even said a word.

"What's shakin'?" he said flippantly, hoping to lure a smile to that too-serious dark face.

"What's shakin'?" David echoed. "Right now it feels like the ground under my feet."

David was definitely not in a mood to be cheered up.

"Okay," Leif said, equally serious. "Tell me what happened."

"I just got back from the police station." David hesitated for a second, then said, "There was a murder down here in D.C. I don't suppose the news will make it to New York— I'm not supposed to talk about it, at least to the media."

"I'll cancel all my press conferences," Leif promised.

"Leif, it was Nick D'Aliso. And I was the one who gave them the ID."

Leif whacked the side of the holo display. "Did I accidentally put this on fast forward? Sounds like I missed something."

David nodded grimly. "I'll tell you the whole story, then you can decide if I'm missing anything—like, say a few bricks shy of a full load."

Leif listened to what had happened to David the night before—and that afternoon. He had a pretty good poker face, but it took some effort to stifle the disbelief he instinctively felt.

On the other hand it was David Gray telling him this incredible tale—Mr. Straight Arrow, the serious scholar. Guys used to joke that if David were picked up by a UFO, he'd come back with full holo recordings and a spectrographic analysis.

Leif lounged back in his seat—he realized he'd almost

leaned into the holo display while listening to his friend's account. "It's pretty wild stuff," he admitted. "I'm glad I didn't have to explain it to my folks—not to mention the cops."

David nodded, his face stony. "Oh, it was fun, all right. I don't think the detective I spoke with really bought what I was saying."

"Well, if you're not happy, we could probably sell the story to some of the people we met out in Hollywood," Leif suggested with a grin. "I can see the holo-feature now." He raised his hands, spreading them apart. "Based on an actual story."

"Dammit, Leif, this is serious!" David's voice rose as his control frayed. "Nicky D'Aliso's *dead.* And somehow he dragged me along for the ride in some weird kind of download. And then there's our dead pal Cetnik. Remember him? I don't need jokes about what's happening!"

"I'm not denying that you've got reason to be worried," Leif said. "But is panicking going to change anything that has already happened? I'd say your cool meter is pretty much redlined right now. Talk it out, pal."

"I need to talk to someone who knows what's going on," David said. "That comes down to either you or the Mac-Phersons. And I can't share anything about D'Aliso's death with them—they may be suspects."

Leif shot up in his chair. "Say again?"

"I thought about it on the way home," David said. "It makes a horrible kind of sense. We know that D'Aliso was dealing with the Forward Group. What better way to deal with a corporate spy than to silence him forever?"

"I get the tune, but I think you're jumping ahead a few tracks again," Leif said.

"You had to have seen it," David said. "I was on holo with Luddie and Sabotine MacPherson when he decided to cut Nicky da Weasel loose. He was trying to hide it, trying to keep cool, but Luddie was plenty angry."

"So?" Leif asked.

David looked worried. "We know that when he feels pushed, he plays rough."

13

For the rest of the afternoon David sat around the house and brooded. His parents didn't actually come out and say it, but he could feel that they didn't want him going out of the house. Just as Detective O'Connor hadn't actually said, ''Don't leave town.'' But David was pretty sure he meant it.

Even Tommy and James were uncharacteristically quiet, sensing that something was wrong.

Something is definitely *wrong,* David thought. First he'd failed to convince the police detective—a friend of Dad's—about that mysterious download. Then Leif had sat listening dubiously as he'd poured out what he'd gone through—and what he feared about the MacPhersons. And Leif was *his* friend!

David gave a great sigh and vigorously rubbed his face. *Could Leif be right?* he wondered. *Am I taking this too seriously? Have I gone off the deep end?*

He lay slumped in his bed, considering the unfairness of the world, when his father came in. Martin Gray's face was serious. ''David, I think you'd better come out and see the news.''

David rose and trailed down the hall after Dad. In the living room the images of two new HoloNews anchors smiled out at him from the display. Of course, as soon as he arrived, an advertisement for a Dodge truck came on.

"What is it?" David asked as they watched an actor who used to play a doctor plug headache pills.

"You'll see in a minute," Dad replied, talking over the promos for other HoloNews shows. Then came a spot for laxatives.

I never noticed there were so many medicine commercials during news broadcasts, David thought. *Is there something about news that makes people sick?*

Considering the knots in his stomach waiting to see what the anchors were going to say, maybe the advertisers had a point.

James wandered in to see what everyone was watching. When the ten-year-old saw the news logo, he promptly headed right out again. The show returned, and the cameras zoomed in on the female anchor, who looked as if she were about to reveal a great secret. Behind her, the logo for "Crime in the Streets" appeared.

"Returning to our headline story, the murdered man found earlier behind a condemned building has been identified. He's a well-known computer hacker, Nicholas D'Aliso, known to his peers as 'Nicky da Weasel.'" A holopic of D'Aliso, giving off plenty of attitude, appeared in the display as the voice-over went on. "D'Aliso, whose body had been stripped of all identification, was recognized by our own Don Samuelson—"

The scene switched to an outside shot. David's stomach knotted tighter as he recognized the alleyway, with the obligatory trenchcoated reporter standing in front of the paint-peeling wall. Don Samuelson ran through the story again, and then narrated as a series of clips ran through the high points—or low points—of D'Aliso's career.

"So," David said numbly, "somebody recognized Nicky da Weasel."

"It will only get worse," his father said with the certainty of years of homicide experience. "When the newspeople only had a dead body, it was good as shock news. 'Look, everybody! There's still crime in Washington!'"

Martin Gray looked disgusted. "But now the media knows it's Nicky da Weasel. They've got a celebrity of sorts. That means the story isn't going to fade. Just the opposite. Reporters will be digging even harder to come up with new angles. And you can bet some hot dog down at headquarters will feed them at least part of your story. It's weird enough to make good copy."

David stared. "But I thought they were going to hold it back," he said.

"Some version will come out," his father angrily predicted. "The brass won't think it's important enough, compared with keeping some newsman—or woman—happy."

David's father proved to be an excellent prophet. After only a couple of hours even the entertainment channels were teasing viewers with a "Download of Death" to get them to watch the late news.

When the item finally came on, it turned out to be more hype than news. They started with a chalk outline in the alley, then went to a photo of Nick D'Aliso. By now the newspeople had uncovered D'Aliso's connection with Hardweare. They showed a clip of Luddie MacPherson with Nicky da Weasel in some flamboyant publicity stunt Nicky'd arranged. Luddie looked uncomfortable in the shot.

When the reporter finally got around to the download, it was almost an afterthought. "Sources close to the investigation say that D'Aliso somehow managed to download information to an associate, the son of a police officer—"

David sighed with relief. "No names."

"Yet," his father said grimly. "If this case doesn't break soon, you can expect to become famous—whether you want it or not."

"Unless a more interesting crime happens to take away their interest," Mom put in. "I'd never wish that on anybody. But—"

She was interrupted by a muted chime.

"Who could be calling at this hour?"

"I've got it!" James said from the hallway. A second later

he came into the living room, giving David a sly look. "It's a girl. She looks kinda upset."

Frowning in puzzlement, David headed to the small holo-system in the hallway. He skidded to a halt before he got within pickup range when he recognized his caller.

She did indeed look "kinda upset."

It was Sabotine MacPherson.

"David!" she exclaimed as he came into her view.

"Just a second," he said. "I want to transfer to someplace a little more private." He heard a theatrical sigh from James behind him as he headed to the bedroom.

David brought up the call on his own system and cut the hallway connection. "Okay," he said.

"I just saw the news." Words seemed to tumble from Sabotine's lips. "Why didn't you tell me—us—that Nicky sent you a message? It's bad enough, discovering that someone killed him—" She blinked back tears, focusing on David's face. "It *is* you, isn't it? I know your dad is with the D.C. police force. And you're about the only 'associate' of Nick's that I can think of with a policeman father."

Reluctantly David nodded.

"Then why didn't you talk to us? Can't you imagine what I've been going through? I've been trying to call Nicky, leaving messages—" Her voice broke again.

"I—I'm sorry." David hated how inadequate those words sounded. "When I realized that the download might be connected with a murder, I had to tell the police. And they told me not to discuss it with anybody."

Sabotine's lips firmed. "Well, you're going to discuss it with me," she insisted. "Nicky and I—we meant something to each other. If there's a last message, I want to hear it."

Her eyes began to flood with tears again. "H-he should have sent it to me."

This is only getting worse, David thought. "It's nothing you'd want to know," he said aloud.

"I'll be the judge of that." Sabotine shook her head. "This is no good. We have to talk—face to face. Meet me at the Musket House Café—do you know it? It's in Georgetown."

"Sabotine—" David began.

"Meet me," Sabotine repeated. "I'll be there at noon tomorrow. Got it?"

She cut the call at her end, and David stared at the dead display in bewilderment. It was bad enough that Sabotine had made the connection from the sketchy information in the news item. But she was pressing him to meet, to talk with her.

One thing David already knew. He could not handle this girl.

He was still trying to gather his thoughts when the system chimed again.

Please let it be Sabotine, changing her mind, David prayed.

Instead, he found himself confronting Leif's image. "I figured you'd be up late, watching the news," David's friend said. "I'm sure you'll be happy to know that Nick D'Aliso's death is national news."

Leif's lips twisted. "That didn't come out right. We're hearing about the murder even up here in New York. I'd think you'd be less than thrilled to hear all this crap about a 'Download of Death.' "

Then it was David's turn to grimace. "I'll never see the news in quite the same way again," he admitted. "But right now I've got worse troubles."

He told Leif how Sabotine had put two and two together— and gotten David Gray as the answer. "She wants to meet me tomorrow at some café in Georgetown—talk this out," he said in dismay.

Leif's response was quick. "Be there," he said decisively.

David was horrified. "Are you crazy?" he demanded. "I would rather wrestle alligators than try to deal with Sabotine MacPherson in the mood she's in."

"You won't have to do it single-handed," Leif promised. "I'll be there with you."

"I think she'd be too much, even for you," David replied. "Besides, are you sure your folks would be happy with this decision?"

Leif didn't look happy, but he said, "I'll clear it with Mom and Dad—somehow. When and where are you supposed to meet?"

"It's a place called the Musket House Café."

"Georgetown."

David nodded. "That's right. Sabotine says she'll be there at noon."

"Then I'll be on the first Metroliner of the morning," Leif said. "I'll swing by, pick you up, and we'll face Sabotine MacPherson together."

"Oh, yeah." David's conflicting emotions showed in his tone. "I hope you know what you're getting into."

"You should be glad for what I'm helping you get out of."

Leif cut the connection, and David headed to the living room to tell his folks that his friend would be dropping by.

Hoping it wasn't a mistake, he decided not to tell them *why* Leif was coming to town.

Georgetown was still Washington's most aggressively quaint— and expensive—neighborhood. It was also a prime tourist destination, as the Sunday crowds along the narrow streets showed.

David glanced glumly out the windows of the taxi he shared with Leif as they rolled down Wisconsin Avenue. "So what is this Musket House place? Another place cashing in on colonial times? Ye Olde Coffee Shoppe?"

"It's not that bad," Leif assured him. "But it's located near that house where the owner used Revolutionary War musket barrels to build his fence."

David gave him a look. "What?"

Leif grinned. "I forgot. Matt is the history buff. And to know about this place, you either have to be into history—or be a tourist."

Sure enough, out-of-towners were pointing at the railings on the fence down the block as the boys got out of the cab. The Musket House Café, however, was cheerfully modern, with big windows, lots of glass, blond wood walls, and comfortable chairs.

Leif deftly snagged a table with a good view of the street, and they settled in. David looked dubiously at the menu. "I've had whole meals for what these people charge for a cup of hot chocolate."

"Fun-on-the-Run Meals from Burger Palace don't count,"

Leif replied. "Besides, it's cocoa, it's good, and they serve real food here."

"You've eaten here before?"

"It's a good nonalcoholic place to hang out in Georgetown," Leif said, browsing through the brunch menu. "We've got a few minutes before Sabotine is supposed to show. Order whatever you like—my treat."

"I'm not hungry," David grumped, pressing a hand to his still-sour stomach.

But somehow, a platter of eggs, ham, home fries, and English muffins appeared in front of him beside his too-expensive hot chocolate. David surprised himself by eating a decent amount of it.

He pushed away his plate, glancing at his watch. "She's late," he said. "Maybe she changed her mind about seeing me. Maybe she's not coming."

"Keep hoping," Leif snorted good-naturedly, his eyes on the crowd passing outside the window. "Hey, there's a pretty girl."

David glanced over and saw Sabotine MacPherson heading for the café's door.

"You can pick 'em," he muttered. "That's her."

Sabotine walked in quickly. She seemed surprised to find someone sitting with David.

"This is Leif Anderson," David said. "He's a friend of mine, from the Net Force Explorers."

The girl reacted a little to the mention of Net Force. "I'm hearing that name a lot, lately," she said. "Luddie has had a meeting with Jay Gridley—and his underlings have been duking it out with our lawyers."

She shook hands with Leif, ordered coffee, then took off her jacket, setting it on the back of her chair as she sat down. "I can't beat around the bush with this. There isn't time." Sabotine glanced at her watch. "I ditched my driver in a boutique I know which happens to have a back door." She managed a wan grin. "He thinks I'm trying on clothes."

Sabotine's expression grew more serious as she focused on David. "I want to know about this download. What did Nicky send you?"

"I don't think—" David began.

But Leif, who'd been watching Sabotine sharply, interrupted. "Tell her."

David glanced at his friend. "Are you sure?"

At Leif's nod, he began. "There was a program icon in my virtual in-box. It activated when I picked it up. At first I thought it was a game—"

He went through the whole sequence of events—the fear, the chase. Running through the memories again, he saw why he thought it was a Hardweare game. The details he remembered came in flashes, overlaid with a heavy seasoning of emotion. During most of the "run away" parts, the background seemed almost like a blur. Only things that directly impacted him, like the wall with its mural, or the splinter, came through clearly.

Sabotine shuddered as he came to the end, nearly spilling her coffee. "And that alley you saw—that fence—those were the same things that were shown on the news yesterday?"

"I can't prove it," David admitted. "The downloaded file just disappeared after the system crashed. But that's what I saw."

"And you think it was Nicky's m—" Sabotine choked on the word—"murder."

Suddenly David was reminded of the Shakespeare quote Luddie had spouted—about how bitter it was to see happiness through someone else's eye. Well, he now knew it was worse to see death that way—through another person's eyes. "He had his vest on. He could have instructed it to upload everything he was experiencing to anyone he knew who was online at the time."

She took a deep breath. "Did you see who did it?

Leif had sat silently through David's recitation, just watching Sabotine. Now he spoke. "You're afraid it was your father—or your brother. That's what this is about, isn't it?"

"I—I'm just afraid all the time." Sabotine pressed her hands against the tabletop, trying to stop their trembling. "Everything is going out of control. People getting killed—"

She made a little noise of distress when she saw her watch. "I've got to go. My driver will be getting suspicious."

Sure, David thought. *That's as good a way as any to avoid questions after you've gotten the information you want.*

He glanced at Leif, who just shrugged his shoulders. They couldn't keep her there.

"I'd like to pay for this," Sabotine offered, gesturing toward their food.

"Don't worry about it," Leif assured her. "We can handle the freight."

She gave him an uncertain smile, thanked them both, then dashed out of the restaurant. She was in such a hurry to leave, she didn't even bother to put her jacket on right. She just slipped it over her shoulders, cape-fashion. David and Leif sat silently watching as she ran out the door.

"Well," David finally said to Leif, "you paid a lot of money for some okay food—and we know nothing we didn't know before."

"We know she's worried that someone in her family might be connected to D'Aliso's killing," Leif said. "And—hey!"

In the crowded street outside a burly man bumped into Sabotine. Another big guy grabbed her.

And the two of them began trying to push her into a waiting car!

14

Sabotine's mouth was open in a scream, but that wouldn't have saved her—except for an unexpected hitch in the bump-and-grab abduction program. The grab part of the team hadn't noticed that her jacket was just hanging from her shoulders.

When the grabber made his move after she recoiled from the bumper, he got the jacket and not Sabotine's shoulders. She twisted free, shrieking like a siren. Both Leif and David bolted from their seats, ran out of the restaurant, and into the street in a flash, ready to confront the would-be kidnappers. The pair of goons had a height, reach, and weight advantage over the boys. But Leif and his friend had both gone through a pretty demanding self-defense course as part of their Net Force Explorers training. Leif knew he was good enough to put a big guy down. He'd done it before.

Right now he could only hope that the Two Stooges were as inept at fighting as they were at kidnapping.

It was beginning to look that way. Sabotine was still loose, still screaming—and fighting, too. The guy who'd initially bumped her made a desperate attempt to grab her in a bear hug. He jumped back, adding to howl to the noise, a set of red claw-marks angling across his face.

An inch up and over, and she'd have gotten an eye, Leif thought. She wasn't bad.

The other guy stood flat-footed, Sabotine's jacket still in his hands. She directed a kick, not to the parts he'd normally protect, but toward his shin, raking it from the knee down and ending by stomping on his instep.

This girl has had self-defense training of her own—the mean and dirty kind, Leif realized.

By now the boys were across the sidewalk and nearly on top of the big guys. The grabber—apparently the brains of the operation—gave it up as a bad job. He jostled his co-kidnapper into the back of the car and jumped in himself. The waiting driver was the most professional of the three. He immediately gunned the engine, and, with a screech of tires, the bad guys were out of there.

Leif jumped back to avoid getting clipped by a fender. In a moment the only signs of the fracas were the still-screaming Sabotine; her jacket on the ground, one arm of the expensive hand-woven material now bearing a tire print; and the rubberneckers staring at it.

Leif reached out and put his arm around Sabotine. It was the most useful thing he could think of to do at that instant. She was clearly losing it—and the fact that she was a remarkably pretty girl had nothing to do with his actions, nothing at all, he assured himself. *I'd do the same thing for anyone that upset.* He looked around at the shocked and staring faces of the crowd surrounding them.

It was inevitable, Leif supposed, that a crowd would gather—all the people attracted by the noise, not to mention the rather agitated café manager who was more interested in the boys than Sabotine—their precipitous departure hadn't included paying the check.

Leif could see David ducking around people, angling into the street while also trying to avoid getting hit by any passing motorists. He returned to where Leif stood with Sabotine's jacket in one hand, and his other arm around the girl's shoulders. She was trembling so badly, it was like holding on to one of those vibrating therapeutic back cushions.

At least she's stopped screaming, Leif thought. *I was be-*

ginning to wonder if the noise would damage my hearing.

"Virginia plate," David reported. "I think I've got it memorized, but I'd like to write it down."

He got his chance as soon as they returned to the café. Leif paid the tab while Sabotine drank a glass of cold water and tried to calm down.

"Whoever trained you did a good job—more important, so did you," Leif complimented the girl. "Is your skill in fighting part of the famous Hardweare security obsession?"

"Personal reasons," Sabotine replied curtly. Then she shook her head. "Sorry. After that rescue, I should be thanking you, not snapping at you." She drew a long, shuddering breath. "One of the first things I did after money began rolling in was to enroll in an antikidnapping course. You see, this has happened to me once before."

David was as shocked as Leif, if his expression was any indication. Leif looked at his friend again. Still shocked. *Well, I guess I heard her right,* Leif thought. *She said she got kidnapped before.*

Sabotine looked at the floor, her long, dark hair veiling her exotic features. "During the court thing—the custody fight between my father and my brother—Dad hid me with friends of his from the Movement."

Even though her voice was so low it was barely audible, Leif could sense the capital *M* on *Movement.*

"Luddie hired people—deprogrammers—to get me out. They did, but it was pretty brutal."

The words Leif had been about to say died on his tongue. He'd been planning to ask Sabotine a couple of tough questions while she was still rattled by the attempted abduction. But now he didn't have the heart. Under her surface calm, he could sense that her internal springs were wound up about as tightly as they would go.

Sabotine was on the verge of flying apart—not surprising after a brisk shot of adrenaline from her struggle and the obviously traumatic memories this new kidnap attempt had stirred up.

"What can we do to help?" he asked.

She looked at her watch. "I've got to get back to that store

I snuck out of," she said, worried. "My driver is probably just about out of patience by now."

With Leif on one side of her and David on the other, Sabotine set off along Wisconsin Avenue, then turned onto a side street. Watching her tense expression as she hurried along, Leif felt a little sad. Here was a healthy, bright, beautiful girl, reduced to an unhappy pawn in a case of family infighting. It was such a waste. Life was meant to be enjoyed.

Sabotine's face was tight with worry as her heels clicked down the block. She turned again, this time into one of Georgetown's mews, a sort of high-toned alleyway. The rear end of a row of quaint old houses now turned into trendy shops faced them. One back door was open. An obviously worried salesgirl stood beside it. Leif could almost taste her look of relief when she saw Sabotine.

"Can I make a suggestion?" Leif said. "Buy a new coat to wear home—so nobody sees this." He gestured to the tire-print markings on the arm of the jacket she wore now. "It might raise questions that you don't want to answer."

"Right," Sabotine said. "Thank you, guys—for everything." She caught each boy's hand and gave a tight squeeze. Then she went dashing through the store's back door, which closed and bolted behind her.

Leif and David were left staring at a solid metal black-painted security door. It had very little in the way of charm. The door obviously hadn't come with the original building, but had been added when the boutique started carrying very expensive merchandise.

"So much for cracking that nut," David said, acknowledging defeat. "So what do we do now, professor?"

Leif turned away and headed out of the mews, aiming for the main drag. "We go where we should have gone ever since Nicky da Weasel got murdered," he said. "We go to Net Force!"

A couple of calls on Leif's wallet-phone determined that Captain Winters was once again spending his free time as an unpaid file clerk in his office. He was surprised to hear that Leif was in Washington, but agreed to see the boys in his office as soon as they could get there.

An expensive cab ride brought Leif and David to Net Force headquarters. Luckily, Leif could afford it.

It was almost a shock to see the captain wearing jeans and a sweater. Even in the informal clothes, he gave the impression of being in uniform. A pile of paper stood by the door. "For the shredder," Winters said. "None of it is classified, so I guess I needn't worry about leaving you two spybusters around it."

Leif could feel the blood rushing to his face. Back in his days in the Marines, Captain Winters had had a reputation for being able to take his subordinates apart when necessary without ever raising his voice. As Leif now could vouch, the captain hadn't lost his touch.

"There's more Hardweare-related stuff we think you should know about," Leif said.

"We've already heard about Nick D'Aliso's murder," Winters said.

"Yes, sir," David said. "But did Detective O'Connor give you the full story about that last download? I was the recipient."

From the look on Winters's face as he listened, the D.C. detective hadn't thought it necessary to share David's story. Winters frowned when he heard about their meeting with Sabotine MacPherson, and his eyes positively blazed when they described the kidnapping attempt.

"Did you report this to the police?" he demanded.

"No, sir," Leif said. "We decided to come to you."

"It's what—half an hour since this incident occurred? There's no chance of catching these guys now."

"I didn't think there was much chance of catching them after they drove away," Leif said. "And Sabotine was much more interested in minimizing the effects of the attempt than bringing charges against the guys who did it. What police officer was going to act on our say-so?"

"I do have the license plate of the getaway car," David offered, digging out a slip of paper.

Winters took it and moved around to his computer. After a couple of orders he glared at the hologram display and threw up his hands in disgust. "Just reported stolen in Fairfax County."

He looked at the boys and tried to soften his tone. "Well, you've gone to the cops, and you've come to me, and you're going to get the same response from me that they gave you, I'm afraid. You can't offer hard proof of anything. The content of D'Aliso's download—even this kidnap attempt—it's just your word. I believe what you say, but I can't take official action."

"Speaking of action," David said, "the guys who staged the kidnap attempt must have been crazy. They tried to snatch Sabotine in a crowded shopping area full of traffic." He shook his head. "Do you think some gunslinging terrorist types have gotten involved?"

"Not necessarily," Winters replied. "Lots of cold-blooded professionals stage kidnappings in urban areas like George-town. It's not so crazy as it sounds. Crowds can help conceal foul play. If that girl's jacket hadn't come loose, she'd have been inside the car before anyone would have noticed. There's an entrance to the Rock Creek Parkway nearby. They could have been heading out of town in minutes."

"That leaves me with the same question I had about twenty minutes ago," David said gloomily. "What do we do now?"

"Well, you got the girl back to her bodyguard," Winters offered. "By now she's probably inside Fortress MacPherson." He looked at David, his glance sharpening. "Did you give away anything you shouldn't have?"

"I told her what was in that download that nobody believes I got," David said a little defiantly. "Otherwise, it was all stuff that was already all over the media."

"Sabotine wanted to know if D'Aliso saw the killer in the downloaded sim, or recording, or whatever it was," Leif added. "She's afraid it could be someone from her family. Her father hated D'Aliso for what he was. Luddie may have hated him for what he could have done."

"I'd say she was a seriously confused young woman."

"But a very pretty one . . ." Leif pointed out.

Winters suddenly grinned as his eyes went from David to

Leif. "Is that so? Well, judging from the looks of you, she's created two equally confused young men."

That got a pair of reluctant smiles from the boys. After appropriate good-byes, they left Winters's office and waited for a cab. Leif stared across the traffic. "I guess the captain was right."

David laughed. "About us being confused?"

"Actually, it was the part about Net Force not being much help." Leif jammed his hands in his pockets. "We did a good deed today, but we're still left with the whole Hardweare mess."

"So, for the third time this afternoon, what do we do?" David asked.

Leif checked his Metroliner schedule. "I guess I go home. You can go up with me to Union Station, or I can freight your fare home."

"The station is fine," David said. "But I was thinking of slightly longer-range goals."

"Oh, it's goals you want." Leif smiled. "I suppose General Directive Twenty-three will cover it."

"And that is?" David asked suspiciously.

" 'Expeditiously achieve opportune ad-hoc objectives in a timely manner,' " Leif replied in his most pompous voice.

David rolled his eyes. "And after that's been run through the translation program for English?"

Leif shrugged. "Wait and see. Maybe we'll get lucky."

David saw Leif board his train, then used the Metro to get home. When he arrived, Mom was already in the kitchen, at work on Sunday dinner. Tommy and James were playing a computer game. From the sounds drifting out of the bedroom, it involved blowing things up—loudly.

Dad was sitting in the living room. When he saw David come into the room, he beckoned him over. Martin Gray had an odd expression on his face. It wasn't the everyday parental "teenagers are a different species" look. David sometimes saw Dad look this way during a tough case. But this time the pain in his eyes was more personal as he turned to his son.

Something was clearly wrong. His father was worried—very worried.

"It was good to see Leif today," David said. "We visited with Captain Winters for a while." That had the advantage of being true, and wasn't likely to stir Dad up very much.

His father nodded, that unnerving look still on his face. "That's better than my afternoon," he said. "Some of my buddies on the job called. Seems there are a couple of suits wandering around, asking questions about me."

"Suits?" David echoed. "You mean detectives? Or Internal Affairs?"

Martin Gray shrugged. "They didn't show any badges, and nobody knew them. When you talked with your friend the captain, did he mention anything about feds being interested in us?"

"No, he didn't," David said. All of a sudden the room seemed strangely cold, as if someone had opened a window and a chilly dank fog were blowing in.

Fog and shadows, David thought. *That's all this case has been so far. Nothing provable, just threats against people— and murder—to get the secrets of Hardweare.*

And now somebody—how had the captain put it? "Some person or persons unknown" was coming out of the murk and going after my family . . . to get a line on me.

I5

That's why Dad looks so funny, David realized. *An official investigation could hurt his career.* It didn't matter that he was an honest cop. Internal Affairs didn't mind getting honest people in trouble, then using them to get dishonest cops. That was one of the reasons why most line officers called them names like "the rat squad."

But if these guys in suits weren't from the rat squad, then they could be after David. Martin Gray's eldest son might be threatened, and his dad didn't know how to protect him.

There was a third possibility. The men could be federal agents, checking into David's background because they'd heard his story about the mystery download—and didn't believe it. That would put him under some sort of suspicion of collusion in Nick D'Aliso's murder—with nobody bothering to mention that he was under investigation.

A sudden spurt of anger went through David's veins. It might be a sign something was really wrong, but at least now the room didn't feel so cold. "No, the captain never mentioned anything to me about feds in the woodpile. But I know one way to find out for sure."

In three quick strides he went over to the living room computer, used its holosystem to make a call to Captain Winters's office.

Winters was surprised to hear from David again so soon. "You just caught me," he said. "I was heading out the door—at last."

But the captain was even more surprised to hear David's blunt question. "Is Net Force or any other branch of the federal government checking up on me and my family?"

"Why would you ask that?" Winters said.

The last thing David wanted right now was a question answered with a question. But he needed answers. He explained about his father's mysterious investigators.

"As far as I know, we're the only agency with jurisdiction in the Hardweare case," the captain said slowly. "Hold on a moment." He gave some orders to his computer, looked at the display, and shook his head. "At this time we seem to be the only guys on the ballfield. And none of our people is checking into your background."

Winters's eyes sharpened as he looked back at David. "Next time these guys turn up, your dad's cop buddies might show off *their* badges and hold those clowns so we can question them."

"I wouldn't hold my breath waiting for that to happen." David grimaced. "They'd probably disappear in a puff of smoke, like the legendary men in black the UFO guys always talk about."

The captain shrugged. "It would be worth a try. In any case . . . be careful, David."

"That's my middle name." David cut the connection and turned to his father. "You heard all that?"

"I heard," Martin Gray said. "And I certainly don't like it." He gave David an almost pleading look. "Is this Hardweare job all that important to you?"

"Dad, I don't think it's about just the job anymore," David said slowly. "I could quit today, and whoever's out there would still come nosing around. There's something weird going on around Hardweare. And anyone connected with the company—even formerly connected with it—is going to draw attention from people concerned about the rumors of leaks."

David managed some kind of smile. "It's sort of like the Tar Baby."

His dad rolled his eyes. "You always had strange taste in childhood stories. I hated having to do that cornpone Uncle Remus dialect when I read to you."

"But the Brer Rabbit stories were actually old folk tales brought over by our people from Africa," David said. As a child, he'd loved the stories of the tricky rabbit and his ever-hungry enemy, Brer Fox. The fox almost got his rabbit dinner when he built a doll out of tar, which stuck to and tangled up Brer Rabbit.

Exactly like this case, David thought. *You touch it, and you never get loose.*

"Maybe you're right," his father finally admitted. "From here on, we take sensible precautions. I'll want to know where you're going and what you're doing. Call in—or at least, call me."

He sighed. "Watch your back. Do I need to say something here about not doing anything stupid?"

"No, sir," David said seriously. "We've already seen what happens when someone tries that."

Martin Gray nodded slowly. "I don't—" He broke off and lowered his voice. "I don't want to see you end up like that D'Aliso kid. Be careful, David."

The two of them stood in silence for a little while. Then Dad gruffly added, "We won't mention any of this to your mother. She worries enough about me on the job." He looked at his son, a half-smile tugging at his lips. "Let her think you're being an especially good son."

David nodded. "I'll try to be that, Dad," he promised. "I'll try."

David might not be able to talk to his mom, but there was one person who'd certainly like to discuss this latest development in the case with him—Leif Anderson.

Briefly David debated calling Leif's wallet-phone while he was still on the New York-bound Metroliner. Leif would get a kick out of that.

In the end, though, David put off the call for two reasons—

both involving privacy. Conversations on portable phones, conducted over the airwaves rather than cables, were much easier to tap in to than secured communications on the vidphone. More important from David's point of view, the only available places to make a call right now were the living room and the hall--both out in the open. If he hoped to keep his promise not to worry his mother, the living room was not a good place to have the conversation he planned to have with Leif.

David let his younger brothers enjoy their gamefest, and then dinner was ready. After he'd eaten and helped his dad do the dishes, David reclaimed the bedroom system.

Leif should be home by now, he thought, so he directed his call to New York.

He got Leif, but in an unusual setting—the kitchen of the huge Anderson apartment. "Mom and Dad are out—the ballet," Leif said. "I'm nuking up some dinner for myself." He glanced away from the pickup to some piece of equipment in the brightly lit room around him. "What's up?"

Leif clearly assumed something had happened to cause David to call him so soon, so he sat down and listened without interruption as David told Leif about everything that had happened since they'd parted company at Union Station. Interestingly, after hearing David's latest story, Leif looked annoyed rather than nervous.

"Sounds like the other side is trying to put on a full-court press—and stick us with playing defense." Leif scowled. "I'm sick and tired of doing that. It hasn't gotten us anywhere."

"It also hasn't gotten us chased down any dark alleys to get shot," David pointed out.

Leif had to agree. "It looks like knowledge is danger in this game. But ignorance sure isn't bliss. Maybe we might swallow our pride and let these humps harass us and our families. But is doing nothing going to convince the people involved that you aren't useful to them? They've killed at least two people trying to get at Hardweare. And what if they don't stop there? After all, they tried to kidnap Sabotine MacPherson."

"Going after Sabotine was an obvious attempt to get leverage on Luddie," David argued.

Then he was hit with a chilling thought. *Suppose someone tried the same trick on me? They wouldn't have to go after Dad or Mom. I've got two little brothers. If they came after my kid brothers, I'd do anything to get them back. And the people behind this have to know that. I may have put my family in danger. I can't just let this ride and hope it will go away.*

If he couldn't get out of this mess, then he'd have to solve it—the sooner, the better.

Leif nodded when he heard David's concerns. "So I take it you're agreed. In this case, the best defense is a strong offense—" He grinned. "As offensive as possible, within reason."

David cautiously nodded.

"We know of there are at least two corporations involved in this leak thing—the Forward Group and Hardweare." Leif shrugged. "You're already in place at Hardweare, so that leaves Forward." He grinned. "And, conveniently enough, their corporate headquarters is located here in New York City."

"We already know those guys are dangerous," David said. "And you—what are you going to do? Go strolling into the lion's den?"

Leif shrugged again. "Guess I'll just have to make sure I'm wearing my steel underwear."

It took Leif a couple of days of intense preparation before he could walk through the doors of the office tower that was home to the Forward Group. This building was located downtown, close to Wall Street, still the Mecca of American capitalism. The lobby was filled with busy people who meant business. In spite of the downturn in office real estate, this building was humming along. It was a far cry from the faded relic housing the Manual Minority's offices.

The Forward Group occupied the top three floors of this skyscraper, so Leif had a long elevator ride to think about what he was doing—now that it was pretty much too late to turn back. He arrived in a reception area that looked like somebody's living room—somebody incredibly wealthy, who didn't mind throwing his money around.

The walls were covered in rich wood paneling that must have come from giant trees—the kind that were supposed to be protected by environmental laws. Soft light streamed from hidden sources, discreetly illuminating furniture that looked as through it came from an old-fashioned, extremely expensive club. Leif stopped to rest a hand on one of the chairs. Real leather upholstery. Hand-carved mahogany frame. Very nice.

A woman sat off to one side of the room at an antique desk which was probably full of high-tech marvels. Considering all the money spent for visual effect, Leif half-expected to find a supermodel working as a receptionist. Instead, a handsome, slightly severe middle-aged woman in a conservative business suit looked at him inquiringly as he walked toward her. Apparently, the Forward Group went in for competent rather than eye-popping when it came to personnel.

"Yes, sir?" The receptionist ran a cool eye over him.

Leif's suit was a good match with the decor—conservative and expensive. Of course, he looked a bit young for the corporate environment. But then, a company who did business with hackers—even on a freelance basis—had to expect the occasional young genius visitor.

"Leif Anderson," he announced himself politely. "I have a meeting with Mr. Symonds."

It had taken some finagling to arrange this appointment. And even before he could get this far, he'd had to identify just who was supposed to run Forward's security organization.

With brisk efficiency the receptionist confirmed the appointment. Moments later Leif was following an attractive young executive assistant down a magnificently carpeted hallway. Along its length doors opened onto expensive-looking offices where men in suits or shirtsleeves did executive-style work.

They came to a door with a discreet nameplate—G. SYMONDS—SECURITY, and the young woman knocked.

Some managers believed in what was called the open-door policy, keeping their offices—and their advice—available to subordinates. Mr. Symonds was apparently not that kind of manager.

Maybe, Leif thought irreverently, *he's in there oiling his gun.*

"Come," a thin voice emerged from a speaker Leif hadn't noticed before.

The young woman opened the door, and they entered an office whose windows offered a spectacular view of New York's harbor. Mr. Symonds was a less impressive sight. He was a shortish, fattish man with a few wisps of mouse-brown hair on an egg-shaped head. Sparse eyebrows, a blob of a nose, jowls like an overweight bulldog's, and a receding chin made up a face that was surprisingly forgettable. Despite Symonds's vague resemblance to Winston Churchill, Leif imagined he'd find it difficult to recall this man's face if he shut his eyes and tried to. The security chief wore the obligatory business suit, white shirt, and boring tie. But even the tie was more memorable than Symonds's features.

Not exactly the image of a super-spy, Leif thought. Then he corrected himself. *Maybe this guy is the perfect corporate agent. A guy like him could walk up to someone on the street and kill him, and nobody would remember what he looked like.*

Symonds's tight little lips quirked slightly in what he probably considered a smile. "Good afternoon, Mr. Anderson. You took a little trouble to find me and make this appointment."

"That's because you're making a little trouble for a friend of mine—David Gray." Leif didn't see any point in being overly polite. "The first thing you should have found out is that he's a Net Force Explorer."

Symonds nodded. "And so are you."

Leif waved that away as if it weren't worth talking about. "Elementary research—not even espionage at all."

"Espionage?" Behind his thick glasses, Symonds's pale eyes—were they blue or gray?—widened.

"Come on, Mr. Symonds. The plate on your door says Security, but I don't think you spend your days worrying over who's sneaking out with extra paper clips. More than anything else, the Forward Group deals in information. You protect that. In fact, if my information is correct, you run a large and expensive organization designed to get information out of other companies."

Symonds said nothing—an excellent information-gathering technique. It led some people to fill that silence with words, and when they did that, they sometimes said too much.

"No, Mr. Security Director, your job is to give headaches to other people's security chiefs. I imagine Luddie Mac-Pherson's head guy is getting gray hair—although he'd feel even worse if he knew about last week's kidnap attempt on Sabotine MacPherson. Shoddy work, by the way. You should hire a better class of kidnapper."

"You have interesting notions of corporate security, Mr. Anderson," Symonds said. "It all sounds very exciting—if I knew what you were talking about."

"Come on, Mr. Symonds. You know. And you're interested in Hardweare—and in those supposed security leaks. I can't prove it yet in a way that'll stand up in a court of law, but I've got enough evidence so far to lead me right to you. Evidence, I might add, that I turned over to Net Force. Besides"—Leif gestured around the office—"why else would you agree to see me if I weren't involved in that messy business?"

"I'm impressed at your modesty, Mr. Anderson," Symonds replied. "The son of the founder and chief mover behind Anderson Investments, Multinational, would always be admitted to this office. You never know when we might become . . . interested in your father's affairs."

Leif almost smiled. "That's just about the most delicate threat I've ever received," he said. "Not to mention a dandy way to turn the conversation away from Hardweare."

"Then I'll talk about Hardweare," Symonds said agreeably enough. "Although I fear you'll find what I have to say somewhat . . . inadequate."

Symonds aimed his colorless eyes directly at Leif—the boring accountant giving a report. "Of course we have an interest in the company. It's small enough to be an easy acquisition, and it controls a quite interesting technology. Frankly, that makes Hardweare a promising prospect for the Forward Group—except for that Net security-leak business."

"And what do you have to say about that 'Net security-eak business'?" Leif asked.

Again, Symonds quirked his lips in his version of a smile. "That whoever is behind it seems to be in the same business as you imagine me to be—although they seem far less picky and far too public for my taste. Too much hoopla, not enough profit out of it, if you get my drift."

"No, I'd guess your taste would lean more toward someone slippery and venal, but somewhat discreet," Leif said. "Say, the late Nick D'Aliso."

"Mr. D'Aliso might once have done some work for us," Symonds said. "At the time he died, however, I believe he was an employee of Hardweare."

"Yet he came to these offices just days before he was murdered."

Symonds shrugged. "Perhaps he was trying to make a corporate sale of his client's product."

"Yeah," Leif said. "He'd have an open market around here."

As he said it, Leif realized something he should have noticed before. Neither Symonds, nor any of the other Forward big shots that he'd seen in the offices he'd passed, wore the current executive status symbol—the Hardweare vest. Whatever was going on at Hardweare, these guys knew something that the rest of the corporate world didn't.

16

After a cab ride home, Leif immediately went to his system to call David. His friend looked a little surprised, until Leif realized he was still wearing his business suit.

"Guess I look a little formal," he said.

"Just a little," David agreed.

"But then, I had to dress the part. Today I talked to our friends at the Forward Group."

David's eyes narrowed. "Exactly who in the Forward Group?"

"A guy named Symonds—head of the Division of Industrial Espionage—although, of course, they don't call it that."

Leif grinned as David's eyes now widened in shock. "What have you done now?"

"Well, he was a little hard to find. This isn't the kind of guy they stick prominently in the corporate directory—"

"No, no." David waved his facetious words away. "You walked into the office of their head spy and did what?"

"For one thing, I told him to lay off you. I told him that we were aware of their movements, that we'd relayed our information to the appropriate parties at Net Force, and we're watching what they're doing closely. Have there been any more mysterious guys in suits turning up around your dad?"

"No," David admitted. "But that could be from Captain Winters passing on the okay for Dad's pals to hold them for questioning—or even from them tapping Dad's calls to his friends."

Leif grinned, looking not at David, but somehow *past* him. It made David look over his shoulder at empty air . . . until he heard the nonsense Leif was spouting. "Hey, you. *YOU!* That's it! Out of here! You're making my friend paranoid. I don't particularly like your looks myself, you big bug—"

"Oh, knock it off!" David burst out.

Leif continued to talk past him to an imaginary holotap operator. "All right. To make my friend feel better, we're going to pretend you're not there."

David rolled his eyes. "Did you give the folks at Forward a taste of your unfortunate sense of humor?"

First Leif pretended to look offended, then he shrugged. "I did ask them a few leading questions."

"And what sort of answers did you get?"

Leif sighed. "I got squat. Bottom line, I'd hate to play poker with these guys." Over David's shoulder he shouted, "You hear that?" to his imaginary listener. Then he turned to David again. "They barely said anything, except for a few choice bluffs. At least," he said uneasily, "I *hope* they're bluffs. Or else my dad may shortly be out of a company to run."

"Leif!" David interrupted. He was really looking worried.

"Look," Leif told him, "I didn't expect them to break into tears and confess every wicked thing they'd done since fourth grade. Heck, I just wanted them to know we knew they were responsible, and that we were watching." He gestured, trying to get David to understand. "It's a start—and I needed a sense of the place. Tell you one thing, though—they're the ones messing with your dad. This guy didn't even flinch when I brought up the subject. He didn't ask what or why. He knew exactly who you were and what I was talking about. They're interested in you—otherwise this Symonds wouldn't have wasted his time with me in that office. He made a speech to the contrary—even a threat to the contrary—but that was simply a distraction."

"Exactly what are they interested in me for?" David said uneasily.

Leif shrugged. "That they didn't say." He grinned. "Maybe they think you're executive material. You may have a future at Forward. They do deal with the hottest technologies."

"Yeah," David said sarcastically, "when they're not trying to run the world."

"So? Work hard, and maybe they'll put you in charge of your own continent."

David laughed. "With my luck it would probably be Antarctica. The weather stinks"—he looked at his dark complexion—"and I wouldn't go with the general color scheme."

Turning serious, he asked, "What did you get from this Symonds?"

"From his words? Nothing," Leif answered. "But there was a lot he didn't have to say. For instance, I didn't see a single Hardweare vest in the Forward offices. Not one. When was the last time you saw a hotshot executive who wasn't wearing one? Now, as a company, they haven't commented on the leaks everybody seems to think are coming from Hardweare—but the executives seem to act as though the vests and leaky security are linked, somehow. Regarding Symonds's interest in you—I challenged him about it, saying that was the only reason he'd let me in his office. Symonds denied that. In fact, he made a little speech, showing he'd checked my background, made little threat against my dad's company. It was the most effort he put into our meeting. You see what I'm saying?"

David just shook his head in wonder at how his friend could read people.

I guess this is how Dr. Watson felt when Sherlock Holmes started making his deductions about people, he thought. *Of course, old Sherlock was fictional. The author could always work things out so Holmes was right.*

David was only too aware that this was real—and deadly earnest. Leif might be betting his life—both their lives—on his reading of a corporate operator who deleted inconvenient people the way David deleted buggy computer files.

Is that how Nick D'Aliso felt at the end? David wondered. *Was his death the result of some sort of computer order? "Batch process. Delete all files with these wild-card tendencies."*

Leif's voice interrupted his thoughts. "How has your end gone?"

"It hasn't," David admitted. "Maybe I lack your nerve, but I haven't had much luck cracking the inner sanctum. Luddie seems to be spending all his time on the Net Force investigation—and Sabotine doesn't return my calls."

"Maybe she's just being shy," Leif suggested. "The beautiful princess is supposed to reward the warrior after he saves her life. It's traditional."

"Just shut up now," David advised, embarrassed. "Besides, I'd think she was more your type. You know, the beautiful, exotic—"

"No way," Leif protested. "She's too high-strung. I like being able to feel comfortable around a girl." He grimaced. "And that's without even thinking about the way she had to grow up."

Leif thought for a second. "That's not to say we can't put our little bit of gallantry to use. You're going to have to go and check a few things—stuff that should be easy enough to find out there in Washington."

David looked at his friend narrowly. Leif was back in scheming mode. "Stuff like what?"

"For starters, the name of that lovely boutique we walked her to after those two clowns tried to stuff her in a sack," Leif suggested. "We only saw the back door, but you should be able to spot the name up front. And speaking of names, maybe you could get one for that salesgirl who helped her. The identity of the owner of the joint would be good, too. And the manager of the Musket House Café—although there you might be able to fudge."

He thought for a second. "Oh. And definitely, you need the name of the bodyguard who drove her that Sunday."

The more he heard, the less happy David became. "What for?" he asked.

"So you can put them together and exert a little pressure

on Princess Sabotine," Leif replied patiently. "Something along the lines of 'Hey, if you can't speak to me, I guess your driver Joe Doakes will have to get an anonymous E-mail about what happened while he was sitting up front in Madame Frou-Frou's. Are you sure Suzanne Shopgirl can be depended on to keep her mouth shut? And which side of the bread you spend there will Madame find the butter on? Yours? Or Luddie's?"

He grinned heartlessly. "Then there's Ms. Eatendrink. She's sure to remember you. After all, we made a pretty dramatic exit to stop that little altercation you were in. She thought we were skipping without paying the bill."

David grimaced. "So, you'll probably get the salesgirl fired, and maybe the bodyguard, too. For what? What are you going to get out of a girl we both know is deeply unhappy right now? You want me to pull a whole bunch of strings, and I don't even think we need to check out Hardweare! You said yourself that you thought those guys in suits came from Forward."

"But the basic problem—the leaks—those do seem to come from somewhere in Hardweare," Leif said. "I don't suppose you follow the business newsgroups on the Net—" He made an astonished sound as David nodded. "No real need for you to know. But put together items in there, and you'd see that Hardweare is in real trouble. If an army marches on its stomach, a business survives on cash flow and credit." Leif looked concerned. "From what I can see, credit is drying up for Hardweare. Whether it's Forward, the whispering campaign, the official investigation, or plain concern about how Hardweare is going to come out of all this, banks have turned off the money taps. In fact, they're calling in loans they already made. Luddie borrowed to get his robot factories up and running. The banks could kill him if too many of them call in the loans now—and someone with deep pockets could come in and pick up Hardweare—lock, stock, and technology."

"What?" David asked. "How?"

Leif sighed at the expression on his friend's face. "Hey, that's business. My dad would be interested in Hardweare if he knew what I know. And he'd probably give Luddie a better deal than, say, the Forward group would.''

''Aside from affecting my feelings of job security, why should this make me want to do what you want?'' David asked.

Leif grinned. ''What a guy! Less than a month on the job, and chock-full of company loyalty!''

But his bantering expression faded as he went on. ''I want you to press Sabotine . . . because I want to speak with Luddie MacPherson.''

''And do what?'' David wanted to know.

''I talked with Symonds to get a look at Forward—and some sort of sense of what they were like. I'd like to do the same with Hardweare. And that means a chat with Luddie.''

''You can't think he's involved in the leaks,'' David said flatly.

''All I know is what I see in the newsgroups,'' Leif replied. ''Luddie MacPherson is fighting tooth and nail to keep Net Force out of his business. Does that strike you as the action of a totally innocent man?''

''It strikes me as the action of a guy who doesn't want his ideas looted,'' David came right back. ''I know you'd like to forget the whole thing, but Captain Winters made a scary suggestion when Cetnik got killed. Remember? He wondered if somebody inside Net Force gave out the information that got Cetnik . . . deleted.''

Leif nodded, looking slightly sick.

''Think how much more the inside dope on the Hardweare vests would be worth,'' David said.

''You make a case for the guy,'' Leif admitted. ''But I still want to talk to him.''

David sighed. ''I'll see what I can do.''

It took David all the blackmail Leif had suggested, plus considerable arguing, before Sabotine even agreed to speak to Luddie.

''I don't know why you're doing this,'' she said, blinking tears away.

''My friend Leif helped save you,'' David reminded her.

"He knows more about business than any six people I know—and that includes Net Force agents. Even though he's up in New York, he knows about your situation—he had to learn, with foreign agents trying to put the screws to him. Most important, he wants to help Luddie—and Hardweare. It can't hurt to talk to him."

"All right," Sabotine said slowly. "I'll talk to Luddie. That's all I can do." She sighed. "He's been so . . . distant lately. It's like he's fighting a war, hunkered down in the trenches, and doesn't have the time or energy to talk to me anymore."

"Just give it a try," David urged.

And if Luddie turns Leif down, what does that mean? David wondered. *It could be what Sabotine said—he's putting his heart and soul into defending his company.*

But David had been checking the newsgroups, designing a search engine to assemble Hardweare news. Every day there were more items, even though the program was designed to kick out the most ridiculous stories.

Net Force didn't believe in trying cases in the media, and Hardweare wasn't a big enough company to cause a stampede of reporters. But stories were getting out, and they didn't paint a flattering picture of Luddie. The stone wall he'd asked his lawyers to create was just short of—or perhaps even beyond—obstruction of justice.

Breaking his usual custom, he'd actually allowed himself to be interviewed, aiming some angry blasts at Net Force in general and at Jay Gridley in particular.

Put it all together, and you begin to get an impression of a brilliant, arrogant . . . and for some reason, desperate . . . man.

David didn't like even toying with the thought. But *could* Luddie somehow be connected to the leaks?

"So, you're the guy who got Net Force on my back." Luddie MacPherson sat facing the hologram pickup as if he were confronting an enemy. It was a four-way connection, Luddie and his sister in their Maryland mansion, David in Washington, and Leif in New York. Things were off to a roaring start.

"I stirred up things to get a little more Net Force activity around Hardweare,'' Leif carefully admitted. ''But I didn't tell them that there was a foreign spy looking for ways into your company, which is what was happening at the time.''

''No,'' Luddie replied. ''You waited for that until the spy was killed and *you* were in the clear. But since Net Force learned about it, I've had their agents all over Hardweare like flies on a cow flop.''

''That shouldn't be a problem,'' Leif replied, ''as long as Hardweare is a bit more savory than a cow flop.''

Luddie's face went white with rage. ''Who the hell do you think you're talking to?'' he demanded. ''I built this company out of the sweat of my own brow. Try that someday, rich boy, and see how you like people sticking their noses in your business.''

''The problem seems to be someone using Hardweare to stick their noses in other people's business,'' Leif shot back. ''I checked the rumor and gossip newsgroups, where most of these famous leaks have been appearing. Today there was one about Jay Gridley's son Mark. It was an accusation, really— that he'd been hacking into places no thirteen-year-old had any business looking at.''

Leif gave Luddie a humorless smile. ''Now, I happen to know the Squirt, so I asked him. He admitted he sneaked into some of the sites mentioned—but Mark's as slick a hacker as you could hope to meet. Even his dad can't catch him unless he decides to confess. There's no way he could have been caught.''

Leif paused. ''Except that he did it while he was wearing a Hardweare vest. Nobody caught him fair and square, did they, Mr. MacPherson? Somehow, your vest leaked the information to somebody, and it showed up online. Besides, why would anyone else dig up a piece of dirt about the son of the man you're going head-to-head with?''

Luddie MacPherson's face was still white, but the color wasn't from livid anger. David could hardly believe it, but the big guy looked . . . scared.

''I can't explain how it's being done,'' he finally said. ''But I can tell you why. There are people out there who want to pick my brains, steal my technology—and then pick my company's bones.''

Luddie was blustering, but his words came faster as his voice got louder. ''Well, I'm not going to let them. I'm not going to let a bunch of government shooflies paw through my designs. Or let their tame scientists dissect my computers and sell their secrets to the slime with the fattest wallet.''

Luddie was out of his chair stalking around. Behind him Sabotine cringed in her seat. ''I'm going to fight, and it's going to be a scorched-earth war. If anybody thinks they can take over Hardweare, they're in for a nasty surprise. There are a few kinks in the design that only live up here.'' He tapped the side of his head. ''And that may be the only information to survive a takeover. I've got it all rigged. The computers are set to wipe, so there'll be no trace of the design specifications. I've got demolition charges set in all the factories. Every production line will go up.''

Luddie bared his teeth at Leif, looking more like his wrestler father than ever. ''Anyone who thinks he's going to win the prize will get—nothing. You tell that to your rich papa, Anderson.''

17

With a shouted order that sounded more like a curse, Luddie MacPherson cut the connection. Leif and David sat in shocked silence for a long moment.

Finally Leif said, "Hmmmmm—that didn't go exactly as I'd expected."

David stared. "You just about accused him of being a criminal. Are you so surprised that he flew off the handle?"

"I needled the guy a little, trying to get a rise out of him. When people get mad, they don't necessarily think about what they're saying."

David just sat there without replying.

Leif frowned. "The scary part is, he *thought* before he said that stuff. He took a deep breath after I hit him with that Mark Gridley tidbit—more like a gulp, I'd say. Then he started on that rant. You notice two things about it? That motor-mouth rush let him stop answering any more questions . . . and then it let him cut us off. I think he planned it that way."

"He did look upset when you mentioned speaking with the Squirt," David admitted. "Stunned, even scared. And what he said after that was pretty wild. But aren't you reading a lot into a single outburst?"

"It's the only outburst we're going to get for a while. We might as well use it," Leif said. "And Luddie knew what he was doing. Why didn't he want to speak to us? Why didn't he give us his side? He's a big boy, runs his own company . . . and he's banging heads pretty successfully with Jay Gridley, so he knows how to handle himself in an argument. But, instead of talking things out with us, he yells—and then runs. Why?"

"I don't know," David said.

Slowly Leif shook his head. "What it looks like to me is the conduct of someone who's guilty."

"You're saying Luddie is using his own invention to spy on users?" David burst out. "That—that's *crazy!*"

Leif gave him a sober look. "Interesting choice of words, there. We've both noticed that Sabotine is—how shall I put it? High-strung? Nervous? Fragile? Maybe we should be wondering if Luddie isn't a few circuits short of a full board, too."

David tried to argue, but feebly. "That's—"

"Don't say 'crazy' again," Leif cut in. "We know that Sabotine had a lousy time growing up. She wound up as a mere marker in the power struggle between her father and her brother."

"Hidden by her father, Battlin' Bob, kidnapped and supposedly deprogrammed by Luddie." David shuddered, thinking of trying to steal James or Tommy from his parents. "That's got to be rough."

"And we both feel sort of sympathetic toward her," Leif said. "Of course, it doesn't hurt that she's a beautiful girl." His eyes took on speculative glint. "On the other side we have bluff, tough Luddie, who divorced his family and lived on his own. What must *his* life have been like before he got away from his father?"

David knew his own dad could lay down the law when he wanted to. It didn't pay to argue with Martin Gray. David had a strong will, but how would he handle it if his father tried to cut something out of his life that seemed as important as breathing? Wouldn't he rebel?

Then, too, David had seen Luddie and Battlin' Bob standing face-to-face. That certainly hadn't been pretty.

"Let's take a moment to look at that struggle between father and son over Sabotine," Leif suggested.

"What?" David couldn't keep the defensive note out of his voice. "Luddie was bringing his sister into the twenty-first century. He felt he had to save her, just like he'd saved himself."

"Yeah," Leif agreed. "But a psychologist would have a field day with the underlying emotions in a conflict like that."

"That's a fine intellectual game, playing armchair psychiatrist," David said. "But we're talking about real people here—and the real world. Would any of the psychological mumbo-jumbo you're spouting explain why Luddie would spy on people who buy his computers? What would he have to do? Write a secret-access trapdoor into the coding on selected vests—or all of them? And why? He's losing money over these leaks, not making money."

"He doesn't want anyone to know how the vests work," Leif pointed out.

"Yeah, but he's got valid business reasons for keeping that secret," David argued. "While doing what you've suggested— that would *destroy* his business—in fact, *is* destroying his business."

Leif nodded, then said, "That is what seems to be happening right now, isn't it? Maybe he gets something we don't know about out of it if the company goes under. Or maybe he isn't completely sane."

David's mouth opened, but nothing came out.

"Luddie is obviously a guy who wants to be in control. He divorced his family to control his own life. He sued his father for his sister, and in the end kidnapped her, to control her life. You told me how he acted when he thought Nick D'Aliso was out of control. Am I making any of this up?"

"No, even if I don't like where you're going with it," David said.

Leif gave his friend a crooked grin. "And then of course, there's that old saying. You know the one. 'There's a fine line—' "

" 'Between genius and madness,' " David finished. "For some stupid reason people use that line around me all too often." He scowled, not wanting to accept what Leif was suggesting. But, he had to admit, Leif had made a surprisingly strong case.

"Right from the beginning, Captain Winters considered this a case of young genius out of control," David finally admitted. His tone wavered between dubious and half-convinced. "Luddie MacPherson certainly is a young genius."

He looked at Leif. "So what are you going to do with your new theory?"

"Do with it?" Leif seemed totally taken aback.

"Are you going to share it with anyone besides me?" David asked. "Like, say, Captain Winters?"

Leif's negative headshake came almost by reflex. "Two reasons," he said. "First, before the captain would act on it, he needs those two little words which he always complains about never getting from us."

"Hard proof," the boys said together.

"And second," Leif went on, "if we treat Sabotine like a piece of cracked chinaware, isn't it only fair to treat Luddie the same way?"

"Feeling sorry let us cover for Sabotine with her brother about leaving her driver and nearly getting kidnapped," David said. "Of course, neither thing would have happened if she hadn't gone to see us."

"You've got a point." Leif frowned. "Whoever is behind this leak thing hasn't just broken privacy laws—there are at least two murders and an attempted kidnapping connected to the case, though it's not real clear who is behind them."

David gave his friend a skeptical look. "And does that mean that Mr. Symonds and the people at the Forward Group are now clean and upright citizens?"

"Oh, the Forward Group is in this, all right," Leif assured him. "Whether they're in up to their waists or up to their necks, I can't tell."

Leif paused for a moment. "As for Luddie—it's not my job to rat him out."

"When we joined the Net Force Explorers, we took an oath to respect the law—" David began.

Leif faced him. "David, the last time I really stuck an oar

in this case and went to Net Force, somebody got killed. I'm not going to go to Winters again because maybe—*maybe*—Luddie MacPherson is not of sound mind. I'll leave it to the professionals to sort it out. If they catch Luddie, I think I'll be sorry for him. I'll certainly be sorry for Sabotine. I'd love to see Net Force nail the Forward Group to the wall, but I don't have anything really solid—or really useful—there, either.''

David felt troubled, but he found himself nodding. "For rich folks, the MacPhersons have more than enough problems.''

Over next couple of days David tried to put the case of the leaking secrets out of his mind. And surprisingly, he succeeded. He had schoolwork to catch up on, and James had a project in his computing class where David was able to offer some useful advice and expertise.

He had finished the last batch of coding compression Hardweare had sent him. And after the warm personal conversation he and Leif had had with Luddie, David didn't expect to see any more work come pouring—or even trickling—in.

So he was surprised to find a download from Sabotine MacPherson when he looked in his virtual mailbox.

My brother can certainly be difficult, her message read, *but I know you meant well. If you're willing to continue working with us, I'm more than willing to keep working with you.*

There were a few snippets of code—no big job, David thought, but apparently a peace offering.

Do I want to go back inside Hardweare? he asked himself. *The money is good, but the headaches have been incredible.* Before he'd joined Hardweare, shadowy men weren't creeping around his family, spies weren't attempting to blackmail his friends. He didn't have to worry whether or not his employer was a mental case. He liked that feeling.

And all those nagging, unresolved questions that clustered around Hardweare? Could he leave them unresolved forever to keep the peace?

Maybe Leif is right, David thought. *It's not my job to find answers. Dad swore an oath to enforce the law. It's the pro-*

fessionals, folks like him, who ought to be digging for the truth.

But something kept nagging at him. *If it's all that simple, so cut and dried, why do I feel guilty about turning my back on the whole situation?*

He sighed, looking around his virtual workspace. Perhaps because space was so tight around the Gray apartment, David had designed himself a large, light, and airy virtual sanctum. There was plenty to look at. One wall, floor to ceiling, was just shelves, containing icons for programs David had bought, traded for, or created himself.

Unfortunately, none of the millions of lines of code represented by those icons could help him now. Was there someone he could talk to about this? He knew how Mom and Dad felt about Hardweare after all this trouble. The only other person who really understood everything that was going on was Leif. And he'd made his decision, bailing on the problem. Captain Winters? No, the captain would be just as glad to have David out of a potential trouble spot.

There we go, David thought. *Four people, four votes for "Run away!"*

It was unanimous.

But still . . .

David jumped up out of his virtual chair. If he let himself, he could argue in circles for hours. What he needed was a decision, quick and clean.

Clean, he thought again, as in clean break.

He picked up an icon that looked like a stylized telephone. The program would let him make a call to any designated hologram system, listed or not. Sabotine had never given him the code to her personal veeyar space, but he had her work number. Of course, it was unlikely she'd be at work at this hour. That might be a plus.

If I catch her in, I'll just explain that life has gotten a bit too hectic to continue working for Hardweare, David thought. No need to mention that Hardweare itself was the main cause of his stress.

And if I don't get Sabotine, I can just leave a message and download the programs back to her.

That was the ticket. Simple, direct, and he'd be out of there.

David activated the phone icon, and a virtual holosystem appeared in front of him. He input the code for Hardweare and waited for the connection.

It can get weird, calling someone who works at home, he thought. Sometimes they answered outside of business hours. For instance, Sabotine had gotten on the holo when he'd called on a Saturday morning.

On the other hand, people sometimes ignored business calls during what was supposed to be their personal time.

David realized he was sort of hoping that's what Sabotine would do tonight. Was there a good holo-drama on? Or even a decent sitcom?

"Don't answer, don't answer," he muttered, then quickly shut up. With his luck, he'd end up getting that recorded.

The connection was made, and David didn't get his wish. Sabotine answered. But this was a different Sabotine from the perfectly groomed girl in the one-of-a-kind outfits. Her face was pale, her hair tousled, and her wide, staring eyes seemed to leap right off her face at David.

"Sabotine?" he said doubtfully. *Oh, man,* he thought. *Did I wake her up? Was this a really bad time to call? Maybe she had a fight with Luddie. . . .*

Sabotine's face was too close to the pickup, making her image too large. It seemed as it she were looking right through David, or peering nearsightedly to find him.

Then he realized her eyes were full of tears.

"D-David?" Sabotine's voice squeaked, and her lips trembled.

"Sabotine, are you all right?" David felt like an idiot when he said that. Quite obviously, something was wrong on the other end of the connection.

"All right . . . ?" Sabotine's voice trailed off as she glanced down at herself. "Yes," she said vaguely. Then she looked back at David and seemed to blink into focus.

"No, I'm not all right," Sabotine said. "Things are very, very wrong here. But it's not me." She swallowed very hard, the image of her face becoming distorted. "David, you helped me before. What am I going to do?"

David was trying to keep up with the girl's sudden changes of mood. Judging by her appearance, what he was dealing with could be anything from an overdose to a nervous breakdown to a reaction to a *very* bad situation, he thought.

"What are you going to do about what?" he asked in his best nonthreatening voice.

"What am I supposed to do about *this*?"

Sabotine extended an unsteady hand to the holo pickup, moving the apparatus. The scene shifted sickeningly, as if David were following along in a sudden focus shift on a zoom lens. The image steadied on what was obviously the other side of a rather Spartan room, set up as a gym. The focus resolved on what David recognized as a weight-training bench with a rack for holding barbells.

Then he made out the bloody figure on the padded bench, the heavy bar pressed down across its chest . . .

Even from where he stood, David could see that Luddie MacPherson wasn't breathing.

18

David tried to shut out the view of the dead body. "Sabotine," he called. "Sabotine!"

The focus shifted again as she stepped in front of the pickup. "What-what-what am I going to *do*?" she wailed.

He tried to speak gently to the distraught girl. "You have to tell the guards," he told her. "And then you have to call the police."

At least it won't be my father's case, he thought gratefully. *The D.C. police don't have jurisdiction out where the Mac-Phersons live.*

Sabotine made a valiant effort to pull herself together. "Yes," she said. "Of course. You're right."

She turned from the holo pickup and walked out of the room. That left David alone with the view of Luddie Mac-Pherson's crushed corpse. He studiously avoided looking at it for the couple of minutes before Sabotine returned with a uniformed guard.

The security man was pale with shock. But he knew his job. "Sir!" he said when he saw David's image. "Were you connected when—did you see what happened here?"

"No," David was glad to say. "I just happened to call Sabotine after—whatever happened."

"We'll have to call the police," the guard went on. "I'll need your name and number. And you should keep yourself available. The cops will probably want to talk with you."

Great, David thought. *Just great.*

"He's David Gray," Sabotine said with some annoyance. She recited his communications code from memory.

"Is that correct, sir?" The guard wrote the information down.

David nodded.

"Thank you, sir. I'm sure you can expect a call."

The guard reached out and cut the connection.

David sank back in the chair where he was seated. Keep himself available for the cops? Why? What good could he do? Luddie's death seemed to invalidate Leif's latest theory on the source of the Net leaks—a theory, David had to admit, that he'd come to believe.

Sighing, he gave his system the code for the Andersons' New York apartment. Leif might as well hear this right away instead of waiting for the news.

Leif's image appeared. Sipping a steaming drink from a Waterford mug, he seemed the picture of well-heeled leisure.

"David! What's up?" he asked.

"Luddie MacPherson is dead," David reported. "I called Sabotine—she'd offered me more work—and she showed me his body. It must have just happened. He'd been working out—doing bench presses—and the barbell fell on him."

Leif closed his eyes for a second. "That's a hard way to go." He frowned. "I have a weird, nagging feeling. Every time we think we've found the villain in this leak case, he's died. I mean, Cetnik pokes up his ugly head and gets it cut off."

"Well, thrown out a window with the rest of him," David corrected.

Leif grimaced. "You know what I mean."

David went on. "Then Nick D'Aliso comes across as a corporate spy, and somebody shoots him."

"Finally, we get Luddie MacPherson, who may or may not be of totally sound mind."

"You were willing to say 'Not!' based on his outburst the other day," David said.

"I wonder why," Leif retorted. "The guy does a nut-job act, threatening total legal war and scorched earth if he loses. Either he's got problems, or some unpleasant secrets he's hiding, or both."

Leif's image glanced hesitantly at David. "You don't think that—he, um—might have done it himself?"

David knew his friend was in shock, asking such a dumb question as that. "If I were going to commit suicide, I could come up with lots of easier ways—and *surer* ways—to do it than dropping 250 pounds on my chest."

The image of Luddie's still form swam up in front of David's eyes, and he shuddered. "It was a bad accident. The weights must have crushed his whole rib cage. It was pretty ugly. No use calling an ambulance. A guard came in there and immediately began talking about bringing in the cops."

Now Leif was getting over his shock. Frowning, he started asking questions. "You say Sabotine had just found him? Weird. Even with crushed bones, you'd think that Luddie would have survived long enough to make some noise. Why didn't he call for help?"

Leif looked sharply at David. "You told me about those workout sessions. Wasn't he usually wearing a Hardweare vest? Was he wearing a vest tonight?"

David thought back, trying to recall what he could of the body he hadn't wanted to look at. "He was wearing one."

"Then there's something wrong here," Leif said. "You told me he used the vest as a trainer. It monitored his physical condition. Wouldn't it have warned him against trying another rep if his muscles couldn't handle it?"

David stared at his friend. "What are you saying?"

"I'm merely pointing out the obvious. Either that vest blew a few circuits—" Leif paused. "Or somebody disabled it when they disabled Luddie."

"It might have been an accident," David tried to insist.

"Maybe he decided to push for one more in spite of what the computer said."

"If it were anyone else, I'd agree with you," Leif said. "But this is Luddie MacPherson we're talking about. The guy believed in his machine."

He put the cup down. "I've got to talk to my folks. Maybe I can swing a ride down to Washington on my dad's corporate jet."

"You're coming down here?" David said. "Why? I thought you were finished plugging leaks."

"I thought I had an answer that I could never convince anyone about," Leif said. "I had Luddie marked down as the bad guy. Now he's dead under—to say the least—suspicious circumstances."

Leif looked grim. "At least we owe it to him and to ourselves to try and find some kind of answer." He sighed. "Maybe this time it will turn out to be the right one."

Leif arrived in D.C. the next morning. He dropped a bag at the apartment his father used when he was in town on business, then went to visit David.

He found his friend hadn't been idle. "We've got to hire a cab for a long ride—your treat," he said. "I was on the holo with Sabotine MacPherson. We have permission to get into Fortress MacPherson and pay a condolence call."

The peace of the Maryland countryside ended abruptly outside the gates of the MacPherson mansion. Vans from several HoloNews networks and even entertainment syndicates clustered outside the closed gates, their microwave masts up and operating. Media types with microphones jockeyed for the best vantage points for their location shots.

Flatprint photographers took pictures of the bedlam, and people from Net newsgroups were setting up portable holo rigs to record the scene.

"What a mess," Leif muttered.

David didn't answer. He was staring at a battered old Dodge parked at the edge of the throng of vehicles.

"Stop the cab!" he ordered abruptly. The driver braked,

and David nudged Leif. "I thought that car looked familiar. It cut off Sabotine's limo when she was with Nick D'Aliso. That's—"

Leif peered through the window and immediately recognized the man behind the steering wheel.

It was Battlin' Bob MacPherson.

Grabbing the door handle, Leif was out of the car in a flash and walking over to the Dodge. David followed a little more warily.

The big man's craggy face looked almost apprehensive as he saw someone approaching. Then his eyes met Leif's face, and he opened the driver's side window.

"I know you," Battlin' Bob said, snapping his fingers to try and stimulate his memory. "Ericsson? No. Leif *Anderson*."

Leif nodded.

"I was pretty rough on you, as I remember," the ex-wrestler said. "Well, here's your chance for payback. I'm asking you—begging you—to take a message in there to my daughter. The guards won't let me through the gate."

Battlin' Bob rested a clenched hand on the door panel. It was a big hand, gnarled, but powerful.

You could easily see hands like those hefting a heavy barbell and dropping it on someone, Leif suddenly thought.

"What's the message?" he asked.

"Just that I'm here," the elder MacPherson said. "That her father will always be there for her."

His voice dropped to a pained mutter. "Luddie's dead, and Sabotine won't see me."

"I'll try to pass your message along," Leif said. "But I can't promise that Sabotine will see me, much less listen to anything I say."

The boys got back in their cab. Battlin' Bob closed his window and sank low in his seat, obviously hoping to be unnoticed.

Leif knew that he and David had no hope of that as their car rolled up to the gates of the estate. Newspeople swarmed around them as David opened the window to present himself to the built-in holo pickup. David blinked as flash attachments flared in his face and microphones where thrust at him.

"Could you tell us who you are, sir?" one reporter asked.

"What's your connection to the MacPherson family?" another wanted to know.

"Please—" an overwhelmed David began. He was rescued as the gates ahead of them opened. The cabbie sent gravel flying as he floored it onto the estate.

He hit the brakes just as sharply when the gates slammed shut behind them.

Three uniformed security types formed a triangle around the car. Two of the guards held automatic weapons—small, but wickedly lethal-looking Israeli submachine guns. The third held a grenade launcher that looked as if it could double as an antitank weapon.

"The car can stay here," the bodyguard with the grenade launcher said. "But all occupants will have to get out."

These guys are tough, Leif thought as he got out and submitted to a thorough search. He noticed that one of the gunners was always in a position to cover them with his weapon.

Once the security guys were sure that they were harmless, the boys were sent on up to the house under escort. Their driver would wait for them in the guardhouse.

He didn't look too happy, but Leif promised him a large tip. "I should be able to afford it," he told the man, "After the kickback I'll get from your boss for getting his company so much free publicity."

Cameras clicked and whirred, and Leif knew that he and David and the cab were the targets of innumerable holo pick-ups.

"If I'd known it was going to be like this, I'd have brought sunglasses," David grumped.

"That wouldn't have hidden your identity," Leif said.

"I'm not talking about that," David replied. "It's those stupid camera flashes! I think I've got little holes burnt in my retinas!"

"It'll fade," Leif replied. "Trust me. I've got long experience with it."

The escorts marched the boys up to the front doors, which

opened automatically, and then conducted them to Sabotine MacPherson's salon.

David glanced around. "Several of Luddie's high-tech toys are already out of here," he whispered to Leif.

Sabotine waited for them in a large wooden chair carved elaborately enough to be called a throne.

Almost as large as her male counterparts, but much plainer, was the female bodyguard who stood behind Sabotine, one hand on the grip of the automatic pistol at her hip.

"I appreciate the trouble you took to come and see me," Sabotine greeted the boys. "Especially you, Leif, coming down from New York."

The girl seemed almost normal, except for a slightly dazed expression on her face.

But Leif had his suspicions that it was all a front. *Does she really think I came all this way to say how sorry I am that Luddie died?*

"It was a terrible accident," Sabotine went on.

"Is that what the local cops think?" Leif interrupted.

"I'm supposed to stop off and see them after our visit," David explained, giving his friend a glare.

"Hey, you're in the clear," Leif said. "You were miles away in Washington when Luddie was found." He looked at Sabotine. "And they'd obviously feel that you couldn't handle that much weight."

She stared at him, mouth and eyes wide open at his manners—or rather, his lack of them.

But he succeeded in shocking a response out of her. "The police said it would have taken a b-big man—someone like my father—"

"He's still hanging on outside, you know," Leif said pretending to ignore the quaver in Sabotine's voice. "Parked on the edge of the media circus, just out of sight from the guardhouse. He said to tell you he was there for you if you needed him. Whatever that means to him."

Shrugging, David fell in with Leif's tough tone. "For whatever good it does, I don't think your father had any connection to what happened."

Leif nodded. "Yeah," he said. "If Luddie were murdered,

it would either have to be an inside job—'' He watched the female guard stiffen as if her pistol had tried to bite her.

''—or someone had the resources to get past all the security—both human and automated,'' David finished.

''The Manual Minority uses some high-tech stuff,'' Leif said. ''I've been on the receiving end of it. But Battlin' Bob MacPherson would need a lot more than what I saw to get in here.''

The guard was staring at both boys as if they were crazy. She looked at Sabotine next, expecting to be told to throw them out.

Instead, Sabotine MacPherson was looking at them intently. ''If this wasn't an accident, then who was behind it?''

''Probably the same people behind Nick D'Aliso's murder—although they'd have had to work harder to target your brother.'' Leif was flying with the moment, talking fast to keep Sabotine's attention, and maybe get her to reveal something. But as he spoke, even he could see his theory made a certain eerie sense.

''It would take deep corporate pockets to pay for a high-tech, professional hit person. We know there's at least one company involved in this whole leak mess who doesn't mind using . . . let's call them extreme measures.'' Leif leaned forward. ''Corporations don't usually get accused of murder. They've got high-priced lawyers to threaten libel suits and keep people shut up. And, if worst comes to worst, those same lawyers can recruit any number of experts-for-hire to exploit any possible ambiguities.''

He looked Sabotine in the eye. ''Accident? Murder? Suicide? Their legal department would have a field day.''

''A corporation.'' Instead of responding to his verbal thrust Sabotine's gaze suddenly became faraway. ''Yes,'' she murmured. ''I can see that.''

Briskly she rose to her feet. ''Not many people around here would have the nerve to say what you just told me,'' she said. ''I appreciate that. And as I said, thank you very much for coming.'' She shook hands, and then was out of there.

The guard who'd brought them up to the house appeared to lead the dumbfounded boys back to their cab.

''What happened there?'' a bemused David asked as they headed down to the guardhouse.

''I believe it's called being dismissed,'' Leif answered. ''But I thought it was only supposed to happen to servants.''

19

David's mother was surprised to see the boys back so early. She offered Leif supper with the Grays that evening, and Leif accepted cheerfully. David couldn't get over how his friend always managed to fit in. He'd seen Leif with powerful political types, or tangling with rich folks, and even with rich, crazy folks like Sabotine and Luddie MacPherson. Now he was in the very middlest of the middle class.

Sitting at the crowded dining table in the Grays' apartment, Leif was the perfect guest. He passed the potatoes, asked David's dad about police work, joked with Tommy, and even made friends with James.

If anything, Leif was *too* successful. When supper was over, David couldn't pry his friend loose from his parents. He wanted to get Leif aside and try to make some sense out of what happened with Sabotine MacPherson that afternoon. Neither of them had been able to make much sense of it during the ride back to Washington.

Instead, Mom and Dad brought Leif into the living room as if he were an adult friend. The younger guys made a fast break for the back bedroom and the computer. Martin Gray sat in a chair, Mom took one side of the couch, and Leif took the other. David was left fidgeting in the middle.

They talked about the world of business and about politics. Dad filled Leif in with what he could about the investigation into the murder of Slobodan Cetnik. David wondered if they would move on to the case of Luddie MacPherson, but the conversation swerved off in a different direction.

Leif looked at his watch. "May I ask a favor?" he said. "My dad's been—how can I say this?—*encouraging* me to watch the HoloNews evening business report. It's coming on in five minutes—"

"Why not?" Dad said. "Although just about all I've got invested is my pension fund."

"It only runs for half an hour," Leif went on. He glanced at David's mother. "Unless there's something else you'd prefer to watch, Mrs. Gray."

Mom shook her head. "No, my programs come on later. Turn on whatever you want. David, why don't you do the honors?"

"Thanks," Leif said, rising with David. "When I call in with my dad later, I'll be able to answer his pop quiz."

David set the system for holographic projection, then tuned in the HoloNews channel. They were just in time. The opening credits, set against real-time stock quotes from the Tokyo market, were just ending. The show's theme music faded, and the image of the commentator appeared.

Funny, David thought. *Business reporters don't have to be as pretty as news anchors—just authoritative.* This guy looked as if someone had stopped an image-morphing halfway between a human and a bulldog. The reporter had a big jaw and firm lips, balanced by intense brown eyes which seemed to glare out of the display.

"Our top story is still developing, as we attempt to obtain confirmations, denials, or answers in general from several major corporations, their lawyers, and law-enforcement agencies."

Behind him a logo appeared—a cracked water pipe, with a deluge coming out, flooding a bunch of stylized people in suits.

"For the past couple of months corporate secrets have been leaked onto the Net—some technical, some embarrassing, some nonsensical. On the whole these leaks were considered"—the newscaster shrugged—"an irritant. But in the last few hours this trickle of information has become a deluge, threatening to wash away the executive positions of several giants of industry."

As the commentator went on, giving names, companies, and details, Leif and David stood frozen in front of the display. David finally realized that, and pulled his friend to the side so they weren't blocking his parent's view.

The cases the commentator ran through were really damaging, enough to cost people their jobs—and many of them years in prison. Bribery, insider trading, stockholder swindles, willful, orchestrated perjury . . . David glanced at Leif when he heard which company was involved in the last charge. It was the Forward Group.

"In the case of the earlier revelations, certain injured parties blamed the leaks on Hardweare vests which executives had been wearing. Since these wearable computers cannot be examined, the charges cannot be affirmed or denied. But the market has apparently come to its own verdict. Hardweare shares have plummeted since this afternoon's disclosures."

The commentator's image grew larger. "Whatever the fates of the executives accused in the latest spate of leaks, punishment is already raining down on Hardweare. Suspicions over the company's connection to the leaks started a credit crunch. Now the death of Luddie MacPherson, Hardweare's founder and main driving force, coupled with the stock crash, seems to spell the end for the innovative company."

David turned to his parents, who sat very still.

Dad turned serious eyes toward his son. "David, I'm very glad you're out of there."

Leif hardly heard a word of the rest of the broadcast.

From what the commentator said, the companies mentioned in the lead story were only the biggest victims of leaks—the tip of the iceberg. Leif didn't like that image—if the leaks continued, they could sink a lot of companies—and hurt the whole country's economy.

From a minor story, something of interest only to a relatively small audience of business freaks, the leak problem had become big news. So had Hardweare. Luddie's death had spurred the interest of the media. The blizzard of incriminating leaks insured more interest—and more coverage.

It wouldn't—couldn't—help HardWeare. But then, the last time they'd spoken with Luddie, he hadn't been interested in helping his company, either. He'd threatened to blow it up. So what was going on? If the company went under, who stood to benefit?

Leif thanked the Grays for dinner, and said he'd be heading back to his dad's apartment.

David walked him downstairs, obviously eager to talk. "This is what you call an unexpected development."

"To put it mildly," Leif agreed. "I was especially interested in that bit about the Forward Group executives lying to the grand jury." He shook his head. "In a weird way, it shakes up a lot of what I believed I knew about the whole leak thing. Everyone's blaming the leaks on Hardweare vests. But that leak couldn't have happened that way."

He ran his hands down his torso, the area where a vest should go. "Remember? I was in their offices. Hardweare vests—nobody wore them. I'd bet they were forbidden objects in the little world of the Forward Group. There's no way someone could have tapped into their corporate councils in-'vest'-igatively."

"Ughhh! The pun is the lowest form of humor," David groaned. "But you're right. Suppose they tapped into the counsels for the defense," David suggested. "There were probably outside lawyers involved in the case. Can we be sure none of them ever wore a Hardweare vest to a meeting at the Forward Group?"

Leif gave his friend a look. "You are *not* making this any easier," he accused.

David grinned. "Just engaging in a little creative paranoia. Have *you* ever worn a HardWeare vest?"

"Once," Leif admitted. "I wanted to check out what it was like."

"You didn't think anything incriminating while you were wearing it, did you?" David asked. "I have to admit, I've been going over what went through my mind the one time I wore one."

"Creative paranoia?" Leif said. "This sounds more like paranoia taken to the red line—and past it."

"Really?" David asked. "How many people store incriminating evidence—stock frauds, decisions to lie in court—on their personal computers?"

"That information is supposed to be personal and private," Leif pointed out.

"Do you keep all your dirty secrets on yours?" David asked.

"Ahm—" Leif opened his mouth to answer, then closed it with a snap. "That's the kind of question a wise man would decline to answer, on the grounds that it might incriminate him. However, if hypothetical dirty secrets existed—no. I'd have to be crazy to trust them where any determined hacker could dig them out."

David nodded. "If you won't leave something on your computer that will get you grounded, can you imagine storing something that could land you in prison? For years?"

"So you're saying the secrets didn't come through the vests' stored memory?" Leif said.

"I think it might have come out of the users' minds," David said slowly.

"Slow down your train of thought, pal! We're about fifty miles past rational."

Leif was trying to joke, but David looked deadly serious. "Remember that download I got? The chase through the alley? We knew it must have been a message from Nick D'Aliso. *But how did D'Aliso know he was going to be chased down that alley and shot? He didn't!*"

Leif stared at his friend. "You're saying the download wasn't a recording."

David nodded again, even more grimly. "I was with Nicky for his last minutes, channeled through the vest he was wearing—*and downloaded through a system he had in place, a system he was familiar with.*"

"So D'Aliso was using Hardweare to spy," Leif said.

"Or he was spying around Hardweare because some third party was aware of the design flaw—or built-in trapdoor," David added.

"Which brings us back to the Forward Group," Leif said unhappily. "For a brief moment there, I thought that maybe we could get rid of them as suspects. Instead, now they loom larger than ever. They'd love to control the source of so many leaks. And with Luddie out of the way, who's going to stop them from taking over Hardweare?"

"After the beating Hardweare took in the stock market, it would be like buying the skeleton of a company," David said.

"More to the point, all this publicity may finally scare people out of wearing the vests." Slowly Leif shook his head. "Now, that would be pretty ironic. The very twist that makes Hardweare a cheap buy for the cannibals at Forward kills its usefulness as a conduit into other executives' brains."

They reached the downstairs door in silence. But when Leif stepped through, he suddenly turned back. "You know the person we'll have to check this with. I think it's too late to catch him at the office, even with his usual awful hours. You free tomorrow morning?"

David didn't even argue. "I'll make time," he said.

Early the next morning Leif tracked down Captain Winters at his Net Force office and made an appointment to see him. But he was told the appointment would have to be later—much later—in the afternoon. As the time approached, he stopped by and collected David. "Net Force, here we come," he said.

The echoing halls of the building were humming with people and purpose as the boys headed for Captain Winters's office. They were held at the door as he conferred with someone via hologram. At last he waved them in.

"I'm afraid this will have to be brief," the captain apologized. "I've been busier than a one-legged man at a butt-kicking contest today."

Winters gave the Net Force Explorers a less-than-nice smile.

"Usually I enjoy this job," he said, "but today I've been torn, boys, torn. I've had to handle the incoming calls. Executives— CEOs, CFOs, the whole alphabet soup—screaming and yelling for Net Force to protect them from leaks that will get their butts fired."

Winters's smile faded. "If I hear the phrase *we're taxpayers* one more time . . ." He shook his head grimly. "And the information we're getting seems to show that these same titans of industry have been working hardest at underpaying those taxes they now claim to be so proud of."

The captain shook his head. "No, right now, I wish I was a full-time line agent again. The rest of Net Force—and law enforcement in general—is having a field day. They're all tracking down the leads that have appeared on the Net—the leaks the companies want stopped. What we've got now will end up in arrests for a lot of corporate scuzzballs who thought they were above the law."

"If they deserve it, they should pay," David said.

"I don't deny that," Leif slowly agreed. "But a lot of innocent people are going to be hurt, too. The damage this will do to business is the kind of economic warfare that guys like Cetnik dreamed of."

"It's going to cost," Winters admitted. "Technology sometimes gets its pound of flesh."

"Yeah." David laughed. "It's kind of ironic. We'll probably have a bunch of former business leaders joining the Manual Minority."

His laugh died, replaced by a thoughtful look.

"We were especially interested in this case involving the Forward Group," Leif said.

"Not surprisingly." Winters nodded. "I've been paying extra attention to that bit of business myself." He shrugged. "According to the leak, it only involves middle-level executives. There's no chance of getting to the sharks in chief."

"When we heard about it—well, our opinions were divided," Leif said. "It could be a genuine leak, aimed at hurting a major corporate predator. Or it could be a blind, with Forward sacrificing a few executives to hide the fact that the company is causing—or at least *using*—the very leaks that are supposedly hurting it."

"Possible," the captain admitted. "This perjury deal, it's not fatal for Forward—unless we get these guys to turn." He looked dubious about the chances of that happening anytime soon. "Of course, they're getting legal representation up the wazoo. But they'd be better off coming over to us for witness protection."

His face lost all expression. "I expect a heavy accident rate among those executives. It will be spread out over time, but things will happen. Car crashes. Electrical malfunctions. Heart attacks. Maybe even a suicide."

"Sort of makes you wonder why anybody would take a job working for a company with such a drastic way of retiring executives," David said.

"Oh, the junior sharks never think it's going to happen to them," Leif said.

Winters gave him a look. "Something tells me you know that mind-set a little too well for my peace of mind."

Leif made a "what can I say?" gesture. "Too much experience with the type. Although my dad doesn't hire sharks—just people who *could* go that way."

"So we still don't have a line on the leaker," Winters said. "And we have a new billion-dollar question. Why this flood of secret information? Why now?"

"From the timing, we'd have to say that Luddie wasn't the info-thief," David said.

"Unless it's a posthumous revenge," Leif suggested. "Usually, that sort of thing happens only in opera or the Bible—you know, larger-than-life gestures by larger-than-life people. *Götterdämmerung*. Samson pulling down the pillars of the temple. Luddie MacPherson's computer program reaching out from the grave to get vengeance on his enemies."

"Or . . ." David said slowly, ". . . Luddie's sister trying to punish the world."

Both Leif and Winters stared at David as he went on. "Leif and I were both too annoyed over being tossed aside to see how she was acting when she dismissed us."

"In a word, she was weird," Leif admitted.

"We've both said it before. Luddie had no reason to wreck his own company by playing with computer leaks. Even though the leaks were clearly coming from within Hardweare, they weren't doing Luddie's company any good—financially or in any other way. But despite the harm the leaks caused him, Luddie's actions with respect to them were those of a man determined to block any kind of law enforcement—he hunkered down behind a legal stone wall when the investigation got serious." David looked at Leif. "He even started that scorched-earth rant. You wondered what he thought he was doing. Maybe that was the wrong question. Try 'Who was he trying to protect?' If Sabotine has been the source of the leaks all along, everything Luddie did makes perfect sense."

"That's as interesting as your theory about the Forward Group." Winters's voice was like a splash of cold water. "Although it's even more off the wall."

"Is it?" David asked. "Name one other person who's intimately connected with Hardweare—and still alive."

Leif glanced over at the captain's hologram setup. "Considering the Forward Group's tendency to be a bit—abrupt—with problems, maybe we should get in touch to make sure Sabotine *is* still alive."

Almost unwillingly, Winters went to his system and made the call. He frowned as the display flickered, but nobody picked up.

"No answer," he grunted. He kicked in the computer and issued a couple of complicated orders. When he saw the results, he started heading from the office. "No connection. But the rest of the local phone system is fine. I'm getting a team and heading out there."

He hesitated, looking at the boys. "Maybe you'd better come, too. Whatever's going on out there, it might be better if she has somebody she knows to talk to."

20

They went in two unmarked cars—low profile: no sirens, no flashing lights. Captain Winters drove, with Leif and David as his passengers, all of them silently raging at the slowness of Washington traffic.

At least, that was the way it went at first. The captain's attitude changed when he made the usual courtesy call to the local police in the township that included the MacPherson mansion.

Whatever he heard from the local cops switched the operation into high gear. Winters got on the horn to the other car, while ordering David to get the flashers out from under the front seat and attach them to the roof. Even as David leaned out the window to set the blinking lights in place, the captain sounded the siren. Coming in the open window, it tore at Leif's ears. An instant later it was joined by the siren on the other car. In deafening duet the cars started forcing their path along the parkway.

Winters steered with one hand, the other cupping the car's microphone. Leif missed the beginning of this radio conversation. All he caught was the end: "—I want those gunships scrambled, and I want them *now*!" Winters barked into the mike. "I may be Net Force these days, but I came out of the Marines—we may need the assets, and we'd better have them in place when we arrive."

The rest of the trip passed in a blur, jockeying past cars that pulled aside for the sirens, challenging those drivers who didn't.

Then they were off the parkway, careening along winding country roads. Long before the stone walls surrounding the MacPherson mansion came into view, they encountered a roadblock. A pair of local police cars were drawn up to re-direct traffic. The local cops stood around looking nervous, their hands on the butts of their pistols.

Captain Winters pulled up and was out of the car, his card case open to show his Net Force credentials. "Anybody know what's going on up there?" he asked.

The sergeant in charge, a big, good-looking guy with a uniform tailored to show off an impressive physique, simply shrugged. "From what we heard, it sounded like a small war—definitely more than we could handle. So we got this glorified traffic detail while waiting for the staties to show."

"I guess you would know." Winters tapped the row of ribbons the sergeant wore over his badge. Leif realized that some of them were military decorations.

"You get these during that last dustup in the Balkans?" the captain asked.

The sergeant thawed a little, nodding. "Sava River campaign."

"I was with I-Corps, holding Corsokak."

The shared battle experience made the police officer more talkative. "We were supposed to hold position here and keep any passersby out of the war zone," he said. "But I went up a little closer—attempted reconnaissance."

He shook his head. "They got pretty incontinent ordnance up there, sir. Something got loose. Either it hopped the wall or flew over and, well, Mr. Wheeler's gonna be pretty upset about what happened to his horse herd."

"Heard and noted, Sergeant," Winters said. "And you won't have to wait for the state police. We'll be going in after the lead choppers size up the situation."

The police officer looked dubious. "You're going to send choppers down into whatever is going on in there?"

"Gunships," Winters corrected. "Marine Super Cobras. They're going to *stop* whatever's going on in there. That's why we'll be able to go in."

As if they'd heard their cue, the long, snakelike silhouettes of the AH1-W gunships appeared in the sky. Winters excused himself and got on the car's radio set to coordinate with the choppers.

As the helicopters advanced, something painfully bright against the darkening sky came whizzing up from the ground. With a deep-throated boom, a blossom of fire erupted beneath the lead gunship, which shuddered in midair, changed angle, and fired a missile in reply.

The explosion on the ground was much louder. It led to a sudden rattle of small-arms fire directed at the gunships. They answered ruthlessly. Winters kept on the horn with the choppers while also talking with the police sergeant, who was on his own radio.

By the time several truckloads of Marines arrived, they had been joined by state troopers and more police.

"Looks like we're ready to go in," the captain said.

The Marines went first, guided by the police sergeant who'd been running the roadblock. Then came the cops and state police, followed by the car full of Net Force agents, and then Captain Winters and the boys.

A thick pall of smoke shrouded the stone walls of the MacPherson estate. It was thrown up by a smoldering grass fire in the pasturelands across the road. The breeze quickened, blowing the smoke away. Leif abruptly turned his head. Clearly an errant shell, missile, whatever, had landed in the middle of the horse herd. Leif was glad the windows were closed and that the wind, judging by the rising cloud of black smoke, was blowing away from them. He wasn't sure he'd want to smell the result.

Winters turned in at the entrance—or rather, where the gate had been. The reinforced steel structure now lay torn, twisted, and partly chewed up, on the ground about ten feet from where it had once stood.

"What did these guys use to get in here?" David asked.
"A tank?"

The former gatehouse was just a mass of masonry rubble.

Several Marines and police officers were trying to clear the collapsed wreckage away. One officer knelt down on the side of the road, rolling out long, black, plastic sacks—body bags.

They continued up the drive to the house. The lawns, which Leif remembered as carefully tended stretches of green, now looked like a battlefield, scorched and scarred with shell holes.

In the distance a tracked vehicle lay on its side, spewing smoke.

"Can you believe it? They did have a tank!" David burst out.

Captain Winters squinted in that direction. "More like an armored personnel carrier," he said. "I can't tell much from this angle—or from what's left. It could be an old Bradley fighting vehicle, or a British Warrior-class APC. One thing we can be sure of, these bozos were playing for keeps."

He nodded toward an area of raw earth where Marines were carefully probing the ground. "On both sides. Looks like some of the intruders were caught in a minefield."

"Great," Leif muttered. "Remind me not to go for any long strolls around the grounds."

The house itself had stood up to the attack pretty well, except for some shattered windows. Sections of the walls bore scorch marks. "Looks like things got pretty hot around here," the military man said.

"I'd say it's still pretty hot." Leif pointed to some of the holes where windows had stood. They still spewed smoke as the furnishings inside blazed away.

"Here comes the answer to that." Captain Winter pulled the car aside, letting a fire engine pass.

In the distance, by the far wall of the estate, rifle fire sounded again—a brief firefight. Then a report came in over the car radio.

"The intruders were having a rough go of it even before our choppers turned up," Winters said. "When their tank went up, they tried to boogie out of Dodge. But it was too late."

His face was grim. "That bang-bang you heard was the last

batch of them. They chose to shoot it out rather than surrender. That's all of them. The site is under control.''

"No prisoners?" David asked in disbelief.

"Apparently, they got one wounded guy. He got his skull creased with a bullet, and he's been out cold. They're bringing him here.''

He pulled the car up in front of the house. Leif noticed that the fancy automatic doors were blown in. Firefighters were moving among Sabotine MacPherson's art collection, trying to save what they could from crackling flames.

Winters got out of the car as a squad of Marines arrived, guarding a pair of stretcher-bearers. The police sergeant who had gone in with the Marines came along, too.

"Has he come around?" Winters asked.

"Just moaning," one of the medical corpsmen replied. "He should start taking an interest in things just about now.''

The police sergeant leaned over the occupant of the stretcher—a hard-looking young man with buzz-cut blond hair. "He's in deep kimchi, but we especially want to find out who sent him," the cop said. "They're gonna be responsible for a lot—''

Moaning, the young man on the stretcher opened his eyes. He froze, taking in the strange faces around him.

"Take it easy, son," Winters said in a surprisingly gentle voice. "You got clipped, but there's no serious damage—''

The young prisoner clamped his mouth shut, apparently grinding his teeth together. Then he grimaced, swallowed, and suddenly began a wild struggle against the bindings holding him to the stretcher.

"Kid, you can't get loose," the cop said.

"He's not trying to get loose!" Winters grabbed the corpsman. "He's gone into convulsions!''

The medical man leaped to his patient, but there was nothing he could do. In seconds the captive—young, strong, barely hurt—lay dead. His eyes were glazed; his face and lips had a faint blue tinge.

Winters came forward and carefully sniffed at the dead man's mouth. "Open it," he told the corpsman. They angled the head toward the glare of the fire engine's headlights.

"There's a broken tooth, or one missing," the corpsman reported.

"The old cyanide pellet in the hollow tooth," Winters said in disgust. "I take it no one searched him all that carefully?"

Although the captain's tone was mild, Leif could predict an unpleasant future for the squad commander who'd missed the poison pill. Leif stared down at the body. This guy wasn't that much older than he was—or David.

The police sergeant shook his head. "That's the sort of fanatic nonsense we ran into fighting those C.A. crazies during my time in the Balkans," he said.

Winters simply looked disgusted. "Or the reaction of a mercenary who's more scared of his employers than of the federal government."

He made a dismissive gesture to the stretcher-bearers. "Take him away. There's nothing we can do to help him— and he's certainly made sure he'll be no help to us."

They spent almost another hour outside the house while firefighters put out the interior blazes.

Had Sabotine survived? David wondered. Some body bags came out—the remains of the hit squad, he was told. Then Winters received a report of more bodies found in the basement—around the sort of steel door usually found in bank vaults. Judging by appearances, the fallen men were a mix of guards and invaders.

"It's either an escape tunnel or a final redoubt," he said. "And I wouldn't expect to find that kind of door on a tunnel."

The door area was pretty chewed up from small-arms and what looked like antitank fire. At last, however, communications were established with the people inside.

There were only a few survivors—Sabotine and her female bodyguard among them. The security woman was pale-faced. A sloppily applied pressure bandage on her arm showed where she'd taken a bullet getting Sabotine into the hidey-hole.

Sabotine MacPherson seemed sunk within herself, almost catatonic.

Winters had David and Leif help her shuffle out. She flinched when she saw bloodstains on the floor. "Dead," she muttered. "More dead. All because of me."

They went upstairs. Sabotine's once-elegant parlor still reeked of smoke. Luddie's wonder-couch was a charred wreck. So was the thronelike chair Sabotine had sat in when she'd dismissed David and Leif.

But the little stool somehow survived. Sabotine huddled on the carved wood seat, as if there was some special comfort to be gained from it.

Captain Winters introduced himself. "Can you tell us what happened?"

Sabotine looked up. "I tried to hurt whoever I thought might have killed Luddie," she said calmly enough. "And they tried to kill me. We heard the explosions at the gate. Our Net connection was cut. Then they were coming through the front door. The security people did their best to slow them down. Matilda and a couple of the guards got me down to the bunker."

The girl drew in a ragged breath. "Matilda got shot. I wanted to leave the door open longer, to let the others get in. But she—she closed it after that." Her eyes lost focus, seeming to stare through the floor. "We saw through the pickups until they were blown out. People dying—so many people dying, all dying because of me."

She flopped to the floor, making a retching sound, but nothing came up.

David knelt beside her, helping her up. "Their job was to protect you," he said. "And that's what they did."

Sabotine glared at him in sudden anger. "I don't mean the guards," she said in that same tone she'd used to dismiss him a few days earlier. Tears filled her eyes. They trickled down her cheeks as she squeezed the lids shut. "I mean Nicky. And Luddie. And who knows how many others—all because I could read people's thoughts."

2I

"Say *what?*" Captain Winters jerked out.

David was watching Sabotine's face. She seemed very calm—*too* calm—as if she'd just confessed something that took a great weight off her mind. But there was the barest flicker of something in her eyes.

He turned to Leif to see if he'd seen it. From the expression on his face, Leif had. Stepping behind Sabotine so she couldn't see him, he mouthed some words at David.

What's he saying? David strained his ears, but all he caught was "between genius."

Then he got it. Leif was repeating the old quote. "There's a thin line between genius . . . and madness."

Fragile, frightened Sabotine. Had her hold on reality finally cracked?

"I'll tell the whole story," she said. "I guess it goes back to when I was a little girl. I thought Daddy was the most wonderful man who'd ever lived—like most little girls, I guess."

Sabotine reached out to David, trying to make him understand. "Daddy said machines were choking the life out of people. Especially computers. And I—I believed him. I believed in what my father was trying to do.''

Her face tightened with remembered pain. ''But Luddie always fought with Daddy. There were a lot of arguments. Luddie's mom had left Daddy, and so did mine. Then Luddie left us. But Daddy and I had each other. He was so proud of the way I learned art and design—working with my hands, not with computers.''

Sabotine shrugged. ''Luddie was out there in the world somewhere, making money. Then he came back—and he sued to take me away from Daddy.''

She sank her face into her hands, as if she were hiding. ''Daddy got me to a safe house, to keep me away from Luddie. But my brother had people find me, and I came to live with him.''

Sabotine peeked from behind her fingers, a look of wonder on her face. ''I thought I should hate Luddie. But then even I could see he was doing something new and wonderful with Hardweare.''

''You thought your father was right, and you thought your brother was right,'' Leif said.

She glanced back over her shoulder at him. ''That's it!'' she said eagerly. Then the spark of animation faded. ''But they couldn't *both* be right.''

''What did you do?'' David asked gently.

''I saw how one could help the other,'' Sabotine replied. ''When Luddie put me in charge of the vests, I added a circuit of my own—I don't suppose he even suspected that I knew how to. It was hard, figuring it out, but in the end it worked.''

''A trapdoor?'' Captain Winters asked in disbelief. ''You just tacked it on to your brother's design?''

''There was nobody to see,'' the girl explained. ''The robo factories put it in every vest. And, as I learned more about computers, I was able to tap in on the processors of Hardweare vests whenever the users connected with the Net.''

''Memos, spreadsheets, dictation notes,'' Winters said. ''You just reached out, and all that information fell into your lap.''

"But it was more than that, wasn't it, Sabotine?" David began to see where the girl was going.

She nodded, almost eagerly. "I thought I could just eavesdrop on all those executives. But when I began downloading, I got much more. I could catch the thoughts and emotions *behind* the things they were doing."

Yeah, David thought, *just like I caught the emotions—the terror that ran through Nick D'Aliso's mind as he was running.* He glanced over at Captain Winters, who sat in silence, appalled at this ultimate violation of privacy.

Sabotine shuddered. "Some of those people were bad—very bad. But it's like I got hooked. I'd tap in on someone, and if I found out something they wanted to keep secret, I'd put it on the Net."

Winters finally got his voice back. "So where did D'Aliso come into this?"

"Nicky came to work for Hardweare, and he found out what I was doing." Tears filled Sabotine's eyes again. "He liked me—he tried to help me, but I—I couldn't stop."

She glanced at David. "When you took the job, he warned me not to talk with you—you'd get me in trouble."

Her hands clenched. "But it was Nicky who got in trouble."

Hunched over, she went on. "We knew some big corporation was sniffing around, trying to find out how the information was coming out—and how to get control of the leaks. Nicky found out who it was. He was approached by the Forward Group. When he couldn't stop them, he tried to play for time." She sighed. "He got them furious by going to them personally."

A wan smile at the memory curved her lips. "About the only thing he *didn't* do was hire a brass band to go in with him. Nicky was sure he'd be seen and connected with Forward—and they'd have to back off."

Her face went desolate. "B-but it didn't save him—they killed him—just like they killed Luddie."

"Why did you let all the secrets out when Luddie died?" Leif asked. "Was it revenge?"

"I wanted to hurt them all—all the soulless monsters who

used machines." For a moment Sabotine fell back into her father's rhetoric.

In fact, David realized with a chill, she even sounded like Battlin' Bob.

"I spent hours on the Net, nonstop, tapping in and blowing out every dirty little secret I heard. But I was really looking for something to hurt the Forward Group. It looked impossible, but then I hooked into this lawyer dictating notes from a client's meeting. They called it shading testimony, but it came down to lying. I put it out, and then those guys came to kill me. They'd gotten everybody else, and they thought with me gone, they could grab up the company."

She looked up defiantly. "Well, it won't get them anything. Hardweare is gone. I've wiped out all the designs and blown the automated factories."

Her voice had shifted again. It was like hearing a female echo to Luddie's rant about leaving nothing behind.

"Luddie always told me there were parts of the design he kept only between his ears," Sabotine finished. "With him gone, no one will ever know how the vests were made. And I've taken care of all the rest."

Captain Winters turned way, feverishly digging out his wallet-phone. He punched in the code for his office and began to make frantic inquiries. "No, I'm not kidding. I want each of those locations checked out. Immediately, if not sooner."

Leif made his way to the room's computer console. He worked for a few moments, then looked back. "I can't tell if it's the fire or what she said. But there seems to be nothing on this system."

Sabotine nodded placidly.

David looked at the girl, beautiful, bright, and obviously, quite hopelessly, insane. Corporate greed had killed her boyfriend the hacker and her brother the genius.

But, David had to admit, Sabotine had shown a certain mad genius as well, keeping her brother's brilliant work out of his killers' bloodstained hands.

Too bad, he thought. Too bad protecting Luddie's incredible accomplishments meant completely erasing all of them.

•   •   •

Sitting in his virtual office, Leif closed out the file marked "Hardweare."

Even in her breakdown, Sabotine had been as good as her word. Hardweare's robot factories were rubble, their computerized records nonexistent. The memory files hadn't merely erased themselves; in some cases, the very media they'd been recorded on had been dissolved. Leif suspected this case would be discussed in business schools for years to come—the most successful large-business lobotomy in history. All that was left were the patent applications. But everybody knew Luddie hadn't put everything he discovered in them.

So, to that extent, Sabotine had been successful. But she hadn't managed to pin the blame for Luddie's murder on the Forward Group. The men who'd attacked the MacPherson mansion were apparently all foreign nationals with no American criminal records—and no fingerprints. They hadn't carried a scrap of identification. Even the manufacturer's labels had been cut from their clothing—which seemed to be foreign and mass-produced.

As weeks had passed, Net Force had managed to get some of these characters identified through Interpol. They all seemed to be mercenaries, people who fought for whoever met their price.

The armored personnel carrier turned out to be equally elusive. It had disappeared from British service during the last round of fighting in the Balkans. Tracking it beyond that point led into a maze of small companies owned by larger companies, which in turn were held by companies that no longer existed—or corporations which apparently had never existed.

As for attempts to reverse-engineer any of the remaining Hardweare vests, the only public results so far had been several hundred of the systems being fried by the antitampering circuit.

Someday, perhaps, someone might be able to insinuate control through the vests' built-in trapdoor and circumvent Luddie MacPherson's tireless defender.

Maybe when Mark Gridley gets a bit older, Leif thought with a grin. But who, if anyone, could ever be able to duplicate the work of that irreplaceable brain?

If the Forward Group killed Luddie—and Leif saw no proof to the contrary—they had probably made a sound strategic move. Left free to pursue his own maverick style of genius, who knows what else he might have come up with?

Luddie might have reinvented the computer—and shaken players like the Forward group right out of the game.

That was what depressed David, Leif knew.

For his own part, Leif was enough of his father's son to regret the missed business opportunities caused by the downfall of Hardweare. The international business scene was becoming more and more hostile to lone geniuses like Luddie MacPherson shaking things up. Entrepreneurial spirit was all right in fast food, or flower delivery . . . or, just barely, in the investment field. But from aerospace to food production, the large and monolithic corporation was becoming the world model. Large, established giants, often with government subsidies . . .

It would be a much grayer world without people like Luddie MacPherson.

Unwilling to contemplate such an unpleasant future, Leif was about to break his Net connection when a complicated series of chimes began. He found the sound less distressing than the sirens or bleeps some people used to catch their interest for incoming data.

Querying his system, he identified the download as a newsfeed of low priority, part of an automated clipping system he maintained on various subjects.

When he asked which file it was headed for, his interest quickened when the answer came back. "Hardweare."

Leif ordered the download formatted for instant viewing. It turned out to be a real-time HoloNews story one of Leif's crawlers had detected on the Net.

It would have been just as easy to break the connection and watch it in the flesh. But since he was here . . .

David answered the incoming message chime on the hallway system of his family's apartment.

A white-faced Leif Anderson looked out from the display. "Have you seen the news?"

"About what?" David asked.

"I guess that gives me the answer," Leif said. "It happened in New York, but this is sure to make the national news. There's been a bomb blast in a downtown office tower." He paused for a second. "It's the building where the Forward Group's offices were located."

"Were?" David echoed. "As in past tense?"

"The report I heard said that the blast ripped through all three floors."

"Sounds like your Mr. Symonds wasn't up to his job," David said. "Or maybe he was so busy keeping an eye on the competition, he didn't bother to protect his own roost." He looked at Leif's image carefully. "There's something you aren't telling me."

"Two things," Leif said. "Then you'll see why I'm not laughing. First, the explosion happened in the middle of a meeting of the Forward Group's management board. The sharks-in-chief may have beaten the rap on Luddie's murder and that perjury case, but this bomb may have wiped them all out. It was set right inside the conference room door."

"I'm sorry. But if you're expecting me to burst into hysterical tears—" David began.

"Nah. I couldn't care less about that," Leif said. "It's the identity of the bomber. Security cameras apparently got images of a guy in a maintenance uniform who wasn't supposed to be there."

He looked straight out of the display. "It was Battlin' Bob MacPherson."

David stared. "You're kidding."

Leif shook his head. "Not about this. Battlin' Bob was shown wheeling a dolly with what looked like a replacement bottle of springwater. Apparently, he wheeled it past the conference room—and his whole shebang went up."

"And him with it?" David demanded. "He was a human bomb?"

"The Japanese had a word for it—*kamikaze*." Leif managed a cynical smile. "As soon as the news came out, there was an immediate response from the Manual Minority. They circulated a signed statement from MacPherson, resigning as president of the organization—specifying 'family prob-lems.' "

The boys stood silent for a moment, Leif's image facing David.

"This one was a mess," David finally said.

"With a big butcher's bill," Leif agreed.

"An entire family, either dead or institutionalized. A prac-tical genius, on the order of Edison, lost forever." David's voice grew angry. "Can you balance that against taking out a room full of corporate predators with a bomb?"

"Bob MacPherson seemed to think so," Leif said quietly. "For me . . . I don't know. I guess only the future can tell."

"Yeah," David said sadly. "Only the future can tell."